ONE DAY IN BUDAPEST

A THRILLER

J.F. PENN

Copyright © J.F.Penn (2013, 2015). All rights reserved.
Second edition.

www.JFPenn.com

ISBN: 978-1-912105-70-0

Requests to publish work from this book should be sent to:
joanna@CurlUpPress.com

Cover and Interior Design: JD Smith Design

Printed by Lightning Source

www.CurlUpPress.com

"All murderers are punished unless they kill in large numbers and to the sound of trumpets."

Voltaire

Dedicated to the memory of those buried in the mass
grave of Dohany Street Synagogue, Budapest

PROLOGUE

THE GUN-METAL DAWN ended another bleak night of Hungarian winter. The sky lightened from pitch black to the colors of bullets and armor, the military might of Hungary's past resonant even in nature, a landscape unable to forget its violent past.

Father Zoli Kovács pulled his vestments closer about him and hurried across the square towards the Basilica of St Stephen, looking up at the grandeur against the backdrop of rain clouds. Although physically chilled, he felt the spiritual warmth of ownership, a pride that came from working at the heart of Hungary's faith. The grand Neo-Classical facade was flanked by two bell towers that stretched into the brightening sky, beacons of faith in a country that had suffered so much. Over the gigantic entranceway were carved the words of Christ, *ego sum veritas et vita*, I am the truth and the life. Father Zoli murmured as he crossed himself, his fingers crippled with arthritis now, but still able to perform his most treasured of gestures.

As he slowly mounted the Basilica steps, he thought that he heard a footfall echo in the square behind him. He turned, but it was empty, with only a few desultory pigeons pecking at the litter left by yesterday's tourists. There were homeless around here, of course, but he felt a shiver up his spine as he sensed something different. After a moment, he shook his head, dismissing his feelings as the wandering of an old man's mind.

Entering the Basilica, Father Zoli paused and breathed in the cool air, the scent of incense hanging like a prayer. Every morning he went through this same ritual, for he felt closer to God in the dark. When he turned on the lights, the splendor of gold seemed to push the vault of heaven far from him, so he savored this quiet moment as a special blessing before he started his day. Sometimes he imagined that the angels guarding the church were watching, that his gentle presence allowed them to drift into the ornate dome and find a place to rest, knowing that he would protect the church during the day. Father Zoli was at peace as he began to light candles around the church, making his way deeper into the nave as the day began to seep in through the stained glass. He stopped to light a special candle in front of the altar dominated by a huge statue of St Stephen, known as St Istvan in Hungarian.

Stephen had been the first King of Hungary, reigning in the early eleventh century, conquering the lands of Transylvania and the Black Magyars, extending his realm and power through battle. As he lay dying with no living heir to succeed him, Stephen had raised his right hand and implored the Blessed Virgin Mary to take the Hungarian people as her subjects and to reign as their Queen. After his death, miracles occurred at his tomb and King Stephen was canonized as the first confessor king of the Catholic church, venerated as the patron saint of Hungary as well as of all kings and dying children.

Reflecting on Stephen's devotion, Father Zoli crossed himself again and headed into the side chapel to check on the holy relic that lay at the heart of the Basilica. As he turned, the candles flickered and he heard a door bang, but the entrance to the church was too far away now to see clearly. Father Zoli debated whether to go and greet the early morning faithful, but he was a man of routine and his duty called.

He unlocked the door to the side chapel from a bundle of keys at his waist and walked through the wooden doors to the shrine. The Holy Right was St Stephen's mummified and incorruptible right hand, the very hand that had given Hungary into the keeping of the Virgin Mary. The brown, shriveled flesh was bunched into a fist and lay upon a bed of scarlet velvet, studded with pearls and rubies. The relic was surrounded by a glass case with a vaulted roof, decorated with gold and silver filigree and protected on all sides by angels and winged beasts. Crossing himself once more, Father Zoli approached with reverence and placed his fingertips gently against the glass. This was the closest anyone could get to the most holy relic of Hungary, a representation of the State itself, precious as both a religious treasure and a national symbol. World War I had seen the decimation of the Austro-Hungarian Empire, and subsequent regimes had oppressed the people, but this hand was a sign that one day Hungary would rise again.

Taking a clean white handkerchief from his pocket, Father Zoli polished the glass, wiping it clean of his prints and making it new again. Tourists paid for the privilege of lighting the shrine in order to take photographs, so he felt that they deserved a clear view.

He heard footsteps and then the creak of the door opening into the shrine. He turned to see a man enter, clean cut, well dressed, with the air of the privileged. His nose was like a beak, his hair waxed to a perfect shine.

"The shrine isn't open to the public yet, my son," Father Zoli said as the man stepped further into the chapel, his hands in his pockets. His eyes darted around the room, but as he confirmed that they were alone, they were drawn irresistibly to the shrine. Father Zoli felt a sudden stab of alarm and moved in front of the Holy Right, to shield it from the voracious eyes.

"I only come to worship, Father," the man said, stepping closer, but in his voice Father Zoli heard an echo of the past, a whisper from the dungeons of the Secret Police where the screams of the tortured drowned out all other sound. Cold fear crept over his skin as two more men stepped into the room behind the first, and closed the door behind them.

"What do you want?" Father Zoli said, his voice breaking as his heart pounded with fear.

"You protect the Holy Right," the first man said. "But what you give to us now, Father, will take the cause of Hungarian nationalism to new heights. St Istvan will be waiting for you with all the treasures of Heaven. You believe that, don't you?"

Father Zoli heard the intent and turned, desperate for a way out. He wasn't ready to go to God yet, and despite his aged body, he clung to life.

The man stepped to the side of the altar and picked up one of the ornate candlesticks, hefting its weight in his hand. Behind him, the other two men fanned out, one taking up a heavy Bible and the other pulling a knife.

"Please, no," Father Zoli fell to his knees, knowing that he couldn't outrun them. "I can get you money, my sons. I can get you help. I'm no threat to you." His voice was hysterical, sobs choking his throat as his desperate fingers clutched at the shrine for divine help.

"Sorry, Father. We need this symbol more than you need your life."

The man stepped in and swung the candlestick like a baseball bat, smashing it against the side of Father Zoli's head. The priest crumpled to the floor, pain exploding, vision clouding. He called out to St Istvan, the mummified hand now obscured by spots of his own blood. It was the last thing he saw as blows rained down and his old body became a sacrifice in that holy place.

CHAPTER 1

DR MORGAN SIERRA STARED out of the window as the taxi from Budapest airport sped towards the city. It was raining and the grey light served to emphasize the monotone of passing streets, punctuated only by the bright neon signs of fast food outlets and sex shops. She noticed banners advertising candidates for the upcoming elections, faces she didn't recognize and words in a language that was alien to her. Morgan smiled, for it was one of the aspects that thrilled her about European travel. Within a short plane ride, or even just a train journey, you could be in a different culture with unpronounceable words, making an adventure of even the shortest business trip.

Morgan had volunteered for the short assignment to Budapest, desperate to get out of the ARKANE headquarters and renew the boundaries of her independence. She had joined the Arcane Religious Knowledge And Numinous Experience Institute with the understanding that she could focus on her own research, but there had been little opportunity for that so far. The last few missions had taken their toll on her body and emotions, so Director Elias Marietti had asked her to remain close to base, and let time heal the scars. But Morgan was restless if she spent too much time thinking, and while her partner Jake was still in recovery, she wanted to get out of the office. She smiled to herself, because that office just happened to be an astounding complex under Trafalgar Square in London, with access to the secret knowledge of the world. Still, it felt good to be somewhere different, even for such a short time.

Her hand rested on a thick briefcase, a discreet handcuff attaching it to her wrist. Morgan touched the leather, warm from her skin, as she had held it on her lap for the short plane flight from London. The briefcase contained two precious artifacts: an early painting by the Jewish-Hungarian artist Béla Czóbel and an antique Torah. Both had been stolen from the Gold Train during the Second World War and now they were finally being returned to the Jewish synagogue in Budapest. Their provenance had been determined beyond question by the ARKANE Institute, and Morgan had volunteered to return them personally.

Morgan was brought up in Israel, her father Jewish and her mother a Welsh Christian. Although she had never converted to Judaism, Morgan knew the pain of European Jewry and wanted to honor her father's memory by being the courier who restored just a tiny part of the plunder. She had read of the history of the Gold Train, one of the many scandals of the aftermath of the war. The Nazi-operated train had been carrying valuables stolen from Hungarian Jews when it was intercepted by American forces in 1945. Many of the owners, nearly 600,000 Hungarian Jews, had been shipped off to Auschwitz-Birkenau to be murdered in the gas chambers, so the treasures had not been returned. After 1946, much of the valuable property was sold and the proceeds given to the International Refugee Organization, but two hundred paintings disappeared into personal collections. In 1998, the Hungarian Gold Train records finally became public and in 2005, the US government had settled with the Hungarian Holocaust survivors, with the money allocated to Holocaust charities.

The taxi pulled up in front of the Dohany Street synagogue and Morgan paid the fare, exiting into pouring rain. The smell of baking and fresh coffee made her stomach rumble, and she glanced at her watch. There was just enough time to grab a bite before her appointment with the Curator of the Museum at the Synagogue.

A few minutes later, Morgan was sitting in the window seat of a small cafe with a strong black coffee and a slice of poppyseed roulade in front of her. As she sipped her dark addiction, the rain eased and through a break in the clouds, the sun illuminated the stunning facade of Europe's largest synagogue. Built in Moorish style, the architecture reminded her of the Alhambra in Spain, with minarets topped with onion domes and striped bands of red, gold and patterned brick. The facade was dominated by a large rose window with the Hebrew script from Exodus 25:8: "And let them make me a sanctuary that I may dwell among them." Morgan had read that Adolf Eichmann had set up his office behind that rose window in 1944, directing the establishment of the Ghetto as he orchestrated the horror of the Final Solution. She shook her head. This area had seen such suffering, but perhaps these objects could at least bring a touch of restitution.

As Morgan finished her coffee and the last crumbs of roulade, the door opened and she heard a faint chanting and shouting in the distance, sirens wailing. A man came in and spoke with the cafe owner in a hushed voice, before going back outside and starting to pull down shutters over the front of the windows.

"So sorry, Madam," the woman who had served her said, with a rueful smile. "We close now. Would you mind … outside?"

"Of course," said Morgan. "I was just leaving anyway. Has something happened?"

The woman glanced out of the window towards the synagogue, her gaze full of concern, fingers clutching the edges of her skirt.

"It's difficult ..." The woman searched for the words in English. "Today, murder at Basilica, there may be trouble ..."

Her voice trailed off but her eyes were fearful. Morgan knew that look, for she had seen it many times in Israel as the sirens warned of an imminent attack. In her years of growing up there, and later as a military psychologist, that expression had blossomed dark on the faces of Jews and Palestinians alike, both sides locked into a Sisyphean conflict. Fear, she had discovered, had no nationality.

Morgan left the cafe as the woman bolted the door behind her and folded inner shutters over the glass windows. On the street outside, a stiff breeze made the election banners wave and crackle. Opposite the shop was a huge signboard advertising the Eröszak party where the handsome face of their leader, László Vay, stared out, his clean-shaven politician's face portraying both strength and charisma. His dark curls were tousled perfectly, his mouth was a sensuous cupid's bow and his eyes, the color of the Caribbean, offered depths of implied pleasure. But the beauty of the man obscured the dark politics of his right-wing political party, Morgan thought. Eröszak was calling for a national registry of Jews and their possessions, a hideous reflection of what had happened here within living memory.

Walking over to the synagogue entrance, Morgan lined up with the other early tourists at the gate for the security check. As the uniformed guards protecting the entrance searched bags, she noticed that they kept looking nervously towards the main road, where the noise of shouting was getting louder.

"I'm here to meet with Anna Bogányi," Morgan said to the security guard when she reached the front of the queue. She was careful to keep her hands where he could see them, used to the rigors of security in Israel. She didn't want to take the handcuff off until the briefcase was safe within the grounds of the synagogue, but she opened the case so that the guard could see inside. The man was distracted, his gaze flitting to the street where it met the main road of Karoly Krt, leading to the city. He glanced in at the contents, the rolled up canvas in the specially constructed box and the Torah.

"Wait," he said, his voice curt. He turned briefly to call to one of the guards inside the metal gates in Hungarian and after a moment, he nodded.

"You can go through."

Morgan walked through the gates into a narrow area that ran across the front of the main synagogue entrance. A thin woman with cropped red hair came forward to greet her, wrapped in a multi-colored patchwork shawl against the pervasive cold. Behind her legs, a dark-haired little girl peeped out, bright eyes shining with curiosity. Morgan was reminded of her own niece, Gemma, for whom she would do anything.

"Dr Sierra. Welcome and thank you for coming all this way. I'm Anna, the Museum Curator."

Her eyes dropped to the briefcase.

"It's my pleasure to be here," Morgan smiled, noting her eagerness. "I'm thrilled to be the courier for this piece of history. And who's this?"

Morgan squatted down so that her face was level with the little girl, who hid her own face in the folds of her mother's skirts.

Anna laughed. "Don't be shy, sweetie … this is Ilona, my daughter. She helps out in the Museum sometimes." A shadow passed over Anna's face. "Today, it's safer for her to be here than at school."

Morgan noticed that behind her the security guards were shutting the gates and instructing the remaining tourists to leave since the synagogue was closing for the day.

"Has something happened?" Morgan asked. "The lady in the cafe across the road said something about a murder."

Anna turned and indicated that Morgan should follow her into the shelter of the museum staircase. There was an undercurrent of tension as Anna glanced behind her, out towards the main street. Ilona ran in front of them up the stairs, her little footsteps echoing in the marble hallway.

As they followed her, Anna explained.

"The news has been on the radio in the last hour. The custodian priest of St Stephen's Basilica was brutally murdered there this morning, and not only that, but the Holy Hand of St Istvan, the symbol of the Hungarian nation, has been stolen. The shrine has been smashed and the relic taken."

"But why close the synagogue? What has that to do with the Jewish community?" Morgan asked.

"There was a star of David painted in the priest's blood on the wall of the chapel." Anna's eyes were hollow as she spoke, as if she saw back into the ashes of the Ghetto. "The Hebrew word *nekama*, meaning revenge, was scrawled next to it."

Morgan frowned. "But surely that's not enough for people to blame the Jewish population before a proper investigation can be carried out?"

"It could be enough to spark the anti-Semitic violence that constantly simmers beneath this city," Anna said. "But there's nothing we can do, and right now I'd rather focus on the joy of the return. The items you bring are finally back where they belong, even though there is no one left of the family they were taken from. Come."

She walked on through the gallery and Morgan followed, their footsteps echoing in the deserted space. The museum was a small collection of religious relics, mainly ritual items for the Shabbat. Morgan glanced into one case at an ornate silver Torah crown, placed on top of the scroll to symbolize its royalty and prestige. She paused to look in at the matching *rimmonim*, or decorative finials, that were etched with tiny pomegranates, reminiscent of the ruby fruit carved into the pillars of Solomon's Temple in Jerusalem. There were also a number of Kiddush cups, embossed with petals and tiny images of the tablets of the Law, used to drink the cup of wine on Shabbat.

"They're beautiful," Morgan said to Anna, feeling a thrill of recognition at the objects, for they were similar to the items that her father had taught her about, reciting scripture as the nights drew in. He would throw his prayer shawl around his shoulders and draw her under it, so that she could settle into the crook of his arm as the Hebrew words thrummed inside her, resonating in his deep voice. She had watched him read from the Torah in the synagogue, using a similar *yad* to this one, the tiny hand with pointed finger tracing the words on the page so that the sacred text was never touched. She couldn't help but smile at the memory.

"That set was saved and kept hidden in the basement of one of the houses designated as Swedish territory in 1944," Anna commented. Seeing the question in Morgan's gaze, she explained further. "The Swedish diplomat and architect Raoul Wallenberg rescued tens of thousands of Hungarian Jews when he was Sweden's special envoy in Budapest. He issued protective passports and sheltered Jews in buildings he claimed as Swedish."

"Did he survive the war?" Morgan asked.

Anna shook her head. "He was detained by the Soviets during the Siege of Budapest in 1945 and is thought to have died at the Moscow Lubyanka at the hands of the Secret Police. He is honored as one of the Righteous Among the Nations, a non-Jew who gave everything for the persecuted Jewish people. We honor him here within the synagogue grounds with the Wallenberg Holocaust Memorial. I'll show you once we've secured these items."

Morgan looked into another display case nearby, containing a silver breastplate decorated with birds, fruit and leaves in an ornate pattern. Worn by the High Priest in the Temple, it hung around the neck of the Torah, protecting the holy words. If only it could have protected Raoul and those who died during that time, Morgan thought, clutching tightly at the handle of the case she carried. It contained so little, but was still important as a symbol of restitution, and she knew that her father would be proud that she was part of this.

"I've got a place for them here," Anna called from further down the museum's long hallway where she was putting on a pair of white gloves. Morgan rested the briefcase on a corner table nearby, finally unlocking the wrist-cuff and opening the case. Anna lifted the Torah carefully and laid it into the padded display case. Her eyes grew wider as she took out the painting and unrolled it, revealing a portrait of a young girl.

"I just wanted to see it," Anna whispered. "But I'm planning an official unveiling and a special exhibition about the Gold Train, so for now, they will just rest here, secure and safe, back where they belong." Anna closed the case gently. "Thank you." She turned and grasped Morgan's hand. "Now let me give you a tour of the grounds. At least it will be quiet now the tourists have gone. Come Ilona."

The little girl skipped ahead of them as Morgan and Anna walked back out of the museum and along a covered stone walkway towards the back of the synagogue precinct. On their left was a garden, mature trees with graceful branches hanging down towards gravestones propped against rectangular bases.

"Of course, it's not customary to have graves within the grounds of a synagogue," Anna explained. "But this area is a mass grave for over two thousand Jewish people who died from hunger and cold within the Ghetto. Perhaps they were lucky to die here, close to home, with those who loved them." Anna continued in a soft voice. "My grandfather was sent to the camps and never seen again, along with so many other Hungarian Jews."

Morgan felt the overwhelming sadness of the place seep into her as they stood in silence for a moment. Where the massive numbers of dead in the concentration camps were difficult to visualize, this intimate graveyard brought home the reality of that time. The names of the dead were engraved in marble and she silently read some of them, the Hungarian pronunciation hard in her mouth, a long way from her father's Spanish ancestry.

The grave backed onto one of the roads at the side of the synagogue grounds and as Morgan and Anna stood there, a rattle and a shout interrupted them. A group of young men loitered outside, their hands on the bars protecting the synagogue's land. A couple of others dragged metal pipes across the fencing, the hollow metallic clang a barely concealed threat, their eyes a challenge of violence.

CHAPTER 2

"Ilona, come now," Anna said, stepping away and walking quickly into the shelter of the stone corridor, out of sight. But Morgan remained, watching the youths as they began chanting something in Hungarian, no doubt some kind of racial slur. She stepped closer to the bars, smiling at them.

"What do you want here, boys?" she asked, her voice unthreatening, her posture open. They looked confused by her advance, obviously expecting her to be cowed and frightened by their threats. "Should I come out there and see if you want to play up close?"

Perhaps they didn't understand her words but Morgan knew they could sense that she was unafraid. She felt a rising outrage and a need to challenge their behavior. Although she wasn't Hungarian, these were her people and this was her land, even though she had never been here before. She would fight, even in a country that wasn't her own, because of the shared history of suffering. This group of boys probably didn't even know what they were chanting about. They were merely repeating slogans heard at the football pitch, or spouted by their parents, racial slurs that were indoctrinated without thought.

Morgan stood close to the fence. They could strike

her from where they stood, but she felt strongly that they wouldn't, that as yet their actions were just bravado. One of the boys looked at her, and she saw fear in his eyes, not of her, but of what the group might do. She tried to send him some strength, for it was individuals like him who could sometimes halt the violence of a group.

The cacophony of a police siren broke the moment and the boys looked around, then scattered. Some turned and shouted back as they ran off, making obscene gestures as they disappeared down the street.

"You have a way with these vandals," a deep voice said, and Morgan turned to see a man in a tight brown leather jacket approaching her. He wasn't tall, perhaps the same height as her, but he was stocky, and she recognized the power of a trained fighter packed into his taut muscles. Morgan sensed in him a reflection of her own tendency to favor action over retreat and she smiled in welcome.

"I'm Morgan Sierra," she said, extending a hand. "I'm here returning some of the artifacts from the Gold Train."

The man returned the smile, flashing white teeth, his jawline emphasized by a line of close-cropped facial hair. He wore a silver star of David as an earring in his left ear and his right cheek up towards his temple was scarred, a pitted surface of puckered flesh. Morgan had seen enough wounds in the Israeli Defense Force to know it was a grenade injury, and she wondered what his story was.

"I'm Zoltan Fischer. You could call me a security consultant for the Jewish community." Zoltan's grip was just a second longer than was necessary, flirtation in his gaze.

The sound of shouting and sirens suddenly intensified and drew their attention back to the entrance.

"You've picked a hell of a day to visit. But come," Zoltan said, "I'll finish the tour with you and let Anna take Ilona inside."

Anna waved to Morgan and hurried with her little girl

back towards the Museum. She was clearly grateful to retreat from the noise and stress of what could touch them out here, preferring to conserve the treasures of the past than face the potential conflict of the present. But that had been the attitude of the community back in the 1940s, Morgan thought, before the Nazis shut them into the Ghetto. She thought of recent news reports in Eastern Europe, the rise of right-wing parties fueled by anti-Semitic slander. There was even a poll in Austria showing that the Nazi party could be re-elected if the ban against it was lifted. Worrying times indeed, and while Israel focused on the threat from Muslim fundamentalists, it seemed that European Jews had as much to fear from their own countrymen.

Zoltan led the way into a courtyard behind the main synagogue. A tree made of metal in the shape of a weeping willow shone silver in the sun, metallic leaves reflecting the light. Around the tree were small piles of stones, placed there in memory of the dead.

"Each leaf on this tree is inscribed with a name," Zoltan explained. "In remembrance of the Hungarian Jewish martyrs. This park is a memorial to all who died in the Shoah, the Holocaust."

"Are any of your family here?" Morgan asked. Zoltan's eyes darkened and he reached forward to touch a leaf with gentle fingers, caressing the inscribed name. He nodded.

"You can read some of their names on the plaque by the mass grave, and there are many more in the lists of those who died at the camps." He turned back to her. "This will always be my fight, Morgan, but what about you? Why did you choose to return our memories to us?"

Morgan closed her eyes for a second, but the light from the tree had seared the names of the victims onto her eyelids, and she opened them again to meet his intense gaze.

"My father was Jewish and I was brought up in Israel. He was Sephardi, from Spain originally, and secular for much of my childhood, but he found his God later in life. I never converted, but when I defend Judaism, as I did in the Israeli Defense Force, I defend him and the right to exist and believe as he did."

Zoltan's eyes were piercing. "So you are a warrior, then?"

Morgan felt the pulsing of her blood against the scars on her body, sustained in fighting against evil. The demon in the bone chapel of Sedlec, the assassins that hunted the Ark of the Covenant, these were battles she would carry forever.

"I thought I could be just a scholar," she replied, "but it seems that I am still called to fight."

The chanting outside was growing louder and more cohesive now, increasing in volume as if the crowd had become a mob. The edge of the harsh words cut through the air, and even though Morgan didn't understand the language, she could discern hatred and destruction in their tone.

"Then I may need your help today," Zoltan said quietly. "I fear that the rabble will bring violence before the truth of the Basilica murder is uncovered."

At that moment, two security guards ran into the square, shouting to Zoltan. He spun and conversed with them quickly, then beckoned for her to follow.

"We are gathering everyone into the main synagogue building. The gates are barred and locked and we've called the police but I fear there will be bloodshed if any Jews are caught outside."

Morgan raced with Zoltan back towards the front of the building in the wake of the security guards. The noise of shouting became deafening as they reached the metal gates that only a little while earlier had opened to a line of interested tourists. Now a mob of around fifty people jeered and roared their anger, faces contorted by hate, shouting for revenge in the wake of the Basilica crimes, rattling the gates as they tried to force their way in.

CHAPTER 3

Zoltan pulled Morgan back against the wall as a glass bottle exploded on the ground in front of them.

"Our community has been preparing for this day," he said. "We knew it would come. We just need to get inside the synagogue and we'll be safe there."

"What about the other people in this area?" Morgan asked, worried for the community.

"They will have locked their doors and pulled down their shutters as soon as the news came out this morning," Zoltan said. "Now we must run across the front to the entrance. Stay close to me."

Morgan smiled at his chivalry, and together they ran the few meters across the front of the synagogue. Bottles and cans were hurled over the fence, and the screaming of the crowd tore the air around them. Morgan could smell rubbish and the stink of feces as offensive projectiles burst on the ground. The doors of the synagogue opened as they approached and then shut firmly behind them. The shouting became a dull roar, but still, Morgan thought with a shudder, the sound of an angry mob intent on violence was enough to make even a veteran soldier afraid.

Zoltan strode into the nave, where a small group of people huddled, some already swaying in prayer. He had a compelling air of authority, clearly ex-military, although he was younger than most of those present. While he gave instructions to those within, Morgan's heart rate began to calm and she became more aware of her surroundings.

The synagogue was immense and fashioned almost like a Christian basilica, with a mix of Byzantine and Gothic elements. Richly colored frescoes of geometric shapes were picked out in gold and red, dominating the ceiling, and tall arches framed the upper balconies. The Torah ark was surrounded by a towering white structure topped with a crown and, unusually for a synagogue, an organ continued the design upwards. It was a beautiful space, strangely decorative for a Jewish place of worship but, Morgan thought to herself, the people here had tried their best to fit in, even with their architecture.

Morgan watched Zoltan as he organized the group, offering words of comfort along with his authority. One old woman sat to the side on a bench, her face expressionless, lips unmoving, staring into the distance. In the blankness of her eyes, Morgan saw that she had been through this experience before, that she was reliving some earlier terror.

She caught Zoltan's eye and moved to join him, speaking in a hushed tone so as not to alarm those present.

"We have to get out of here," she said. "We need to find the Holy Right and return it to the Basilica, because if this continues into the night, I fear for these people."

Zoltan's eyes were hard. "And who are you, Morgan Sierra, to be of any use to me in this place?"

Morgan met his gaze without flinching. "I know you must have a way out, and you need a partner who can operate in the field. You have to leave your security guards on duty here to protect these people and I can be useful, so put me to work." She paused, laying her hand on his arm. "This is what I do, Zoltan. I find religious objects and I fight bad guys."

A glimmer of humor shone in his eyes. "And today,

Budapest harbors these bad guys?"

Morgan nodded. "Do you have weapons here?"

Zoltan hesitated, looking back at the group. They were mainly academics and older people who volunteered at the synagogue. Morgan saw Anna comforting one woman, rocking her in her arms and stroking her hair as Ilona sat close by, eyes wide with fear.

He shook his head slowly, and Morgan saw resignation in his eyes.

"Follow me."

In one corner of the synagogue was an ornate screen. Zoltan stepped behind it and tapped into a keypad on the wall. The heavy door clicked and he pushed it open to reveal a smaller courtyard outside protected by high walls but still open to the sky. A large metal storage container loomed in the shadows.

"This area is just outside the holy ground of the synagogue," Zoltan explained. "But we keep the store close just in case."

He tapped in another code and pulled open the door, gesturing for Morgan to enter. There were several racks of guns, old but clean, and clearly well serviced. Morgan picked up a Glock 17 handgun.

"Austrian," Zoltan said. "Military issue."

"Thinking about it, I'm not sure that we should take weapons," Morgan said. "We need to stay out of sight as much as possible. If we get stopped, carrying guns will get us arrested, which won't help anyone here."

"Agreed," Zoltan said, picking up a tire iron from a pile of tools, hefting its weight in his hand. "This will have to do." He put it into a backpack with a couple of torches and some other basic equipment. "Our only chance to stop a riot tonight is to find the Hand." He picked up a protective vest. "But will you wear this, just in case? It's a spare."

Morgan nodded, reaching for it. Zoltan stripped off his

own jacket and shirt, revealing a trim, muscled torso clad in a tight, white t-shirt, a criss-cross of white scars emerging from his right sleeve and continuing down his arm. Morgan watched for a second, resisting the urge to touch him, before pulling off her own coat and sweater, feeling the tension in her muscles. It felt good to move, the adrenalin pulsing through her. She claimed to be an academic, but this life of action suited her. By his eyes on her toned body, it was clear Zoltan thought so too. Their eyes met, danger sparking an attraction, then Zoltan broke the gaze as he zipped up the small backpack and they stepped from the lock-up.

"There's a tunnel we can use to get out of here," he said, re-entering the code to secure the container. "It emerges a few streets away in the basement of a bar where we have friends."

A wailing scream came from the main synagogue and Zoltan dashed back inside. Morgan followed after him to find that the old woman who had sat in catatonic silence had broken down in hysterical weeping.

"We must go now," Zoltan said, his face stony, fists clenched. "I will not allow my people to go through this again."

He led Morgan to a corridor that ran behind the *aron ha-kodesh*, the Holy Ark that held the Torah scrolls, and then into a small square room lined with books.

"Now we go down," Zoltan said, pulling aside a rug that concealed a trapdoor. He tugged it up revealing a dark and narrow hole. Morgan's thoughts flashed to the mass grave outside, the bodies of those starved to death lowered into pits like this. Zoltan stepped down onto the ladder and then passed her up a head torch. "It's not too far. My men have orders to bring the others this way if the synagogue wall is breached, but I fear that the elderly would struggle to escape down here."

He disappeared into the hole and Morgan watched him

descend. She took a deep breath and followed him, climbing down about six feet. Zoltan was waiting at the bottom in a low tunnel, and as soon as Morgan's feet touched the ground, he set off into the darkness, the light from his head torch illuminating dank earth reinforced with wooden planks. With barely enough room to stand upright, Morgan had to bend to walk quickly behind him.

It must have been built after the Ghetto, Morgan thought, as back then these blocks would have been surrounded by a high fence and stone wall. No food had been allowed in, and rubbish, waste and dead bodies had lain on the streets unable to be collected. She walked faster, specters of the past chasing her through the dark tunnel, the bony fingers of the dead crying out for justice while the living wailed in the synagogue behind her. She felt claustrophobic, as if the very earth wanted to crush her. There was a light touch on her cheek and she let out a little noise of alarm.

"Are you OK?" Zoltan's whisper came back and he shone his torch at her feet.

Morgan touched her face, wiping away a crumbling flake of earth.

"Yes, sorry, just a bit jumpy."

"Only a little further." He turned and they walked on until they reached another ladder, which Zoltan quickly climbed, pushing open the hatch above. Light flooded down into the pit as Zoltan reached down to help Morgan up. They emerged into a beer cellar in the basement of a local pub, with metal barrels piled up in one corner, the smell of hops in the air.

"We need to find out more about the ultra right-wing Nationalist groups," Zoltan said. "The relic theft is not the work of Jewish groups, but of a faction trying to stir up violence for their own agenda. With the elections only a few days away, there are those who would benefit greatly from a backlash against the Jews and a resurgence of Hungarian nationalism. I know someone who can help us … but you're not going to like where he works."

CHAPTER 4

IN ANOTHER AREA OF Budapest, the Jewish delicatessen of Erzsébetváros was busy, full of people gossiping about the murder at the Basilica, their voices a hubbub of interest tinged with fear. Alma Kadosa served a customer with fresh bread, wrapping it quickly with fast hands, unconscious of the actions she had performed so many times before. She heard snippets of conversation, rumors of a mob calling for blood and vengeance and she felt a dart of concern for her parents, who were at the synagogue. She would call them as soon as the shop quietened down. They were still faithful to a religion into which she had been born but didn't really identify with. Alma was proudly Hungarian first, embracing all the opportunities the country offered hardworking young people. She only had to save a few hundred more forints and then she could afford her dream holiday, visiting the famous art galleries of Italy and France that she studied at night school.

Suddenly, the sound of revving engines interrupted Alma's thoughts and stilled the conversation around her. Brakes squealed to a halt and Alma could see men jumping out of a white van. There was shouting and the atmosphere in the shop shifted. Alma watched the old people shrink into themselves, some sinking silently behind display units as if they instinctively knew what was coming.

"Quickly," hissed Ferenc, the portly owner of the store, as he pushed open the back door of the shop and urged some of the customers to flee. Those closest to the door ran, leaving shopping bags full on the ground. Alma was trapped behind the bread counter and, although she felt fearful, she also didn't understand what was going on. How could there be a threat to their little shop?

She remained standing as the door banged open and, one after another, five men entered, their faces set in a sneer of malevolence, eyes shining with a lust for violence. Two carried baseball bats that they thumped from one hand to another and the others held guns in a relaxed grip.

Their leader strode in behind them, his eyes obscured by sunglasses. His nose was sharp, like a beak, and his dark hair shone with wax styling. He was closely shaven and Alma could smell the spicy cologne that he exuded along with an air of sophisticated violence. His eyes fell on her and Alma felt her heart pound in fear and her muscles tighten.

He walked forward, his eyes fixed on hers, while his men stood silently to one side as if waiting for a signal.

"What are you looking at, Jew-bitch?" he asked, his voice almost an obscene caress and his mouth curving into a smile. Alma could read his intent, and her hand gripped the bread-knife in front of her. She thought of her grandparents, survivors of the camps, and her parents who had suffered under the Soviets. This was her fight now, and suddenly she felt proud of her heritage. She would not deny who she was, even though she had spent her lifetime avoiding the synagogue and her parents' religious fervor.

"Can I help you, gentlemen?" Alma asked, her voice shaky. Out of the corner of her eye, she could see the customers frozen with fear. Nearest was old Mrs Karolyi with her gnarled hands who came in every day for fresh poppyseed cake. Her eyes were closed and her chest was heaving, as if she was having a panic attack. Behind her was a mother, clutching her young son to her chest, hiding his eyes and looking away, hoping that by not seeing what was happening, they would avoid the oncoming threat.

"You Jews have helped yourselves for far too long," the man snarled at Alma. "And now you have stolen the symbol of our country, the Holy Right, no doubt for some disgusting ritual." He came close to the counter and leaned over it towards Alma. Everything in her wanted to thrust the bread knife at him, but she knew that his jacket would stop the blade and then she feared he would use the knife on her. Her heart pounded.

"We don't know anything about the Holy Right. We are Hungarian, just like you." Alma's voice trembled and the man smiled, his grin wolfish. He raised a hand and slapped her face hard, the crack resounding in the shop. Anna felt the pain a split second after the noise, her hand flying to her cheek and tears springing to her eyes.

"Don't you dare claim to be Magyar," he snarled. "You are nothing, and we will show you what you are worth."

He signaled behind him and the other men started laying into the shelving and displays with their bats, smashing glass cases and bottles. The smell of pickled vegetables filled the air and the screams of the frightened customers were lost amongst the violent outburst. Alma heard Ferenc moaning from behind his till, shaking his head as his livelihood was destroyed, the perfect little shop with everything in its place smashed to pieces. Glass shards rained down on the customers, but although the men heaved their bats down right next to the people huddled on the floor, they didn't hit anyone. Alma was shaking with shock and fear now. Could this really be happening in twenty-first century Hungary?

"Today we are taking vengeance for the stolen Holy Right," the man said. "But beating you to death doesn't give the correct signal to the Jewish community. We want to cast a longer shadow into the past today." He grinned and cupped Alma's chin roughly in his bony hand. "You're pretty, little Jewess. I'll take you for sure, but we need several more for our little enactment. Will you choose, or shall I?"

Alma stared into his eyes, dark pools showing no acknowledgment of her humanity. "You can't do this," she said. "The police will be here any minute. They'll stop you."

He laughed. "Haven't you noticed, idiot Jews?" He spun and addressed the cowering shop customers. "The police aren't interested in you, they only care about defending Hungary. And today, we're doing their job for them."

He barked a command and each of the men grabbed one of the customers.

"Now, Jewess, will you come quietly or shall I take someone else?"

The man turned and his eyes fixed on the mother with her young son, and old Mrs Karolyi. He moved towards them and the old woman opened her eyes, a piercing blue that fixed on his.

"Shame on you," she whispered. "You bring dishonor to Hungary. This brutality should have died with the generation that started it."

The man laughed at her and then his face transformed.

"It is you who bring shame." He spat at the old woman. "We bring glory, for we are ridding this country of the unwanted Jews, Roma and dirty foreigners. Soon, we Magyar will be great again."

He reached for a tin of pickled gherkins from the shelf and used it to smash Mrs Karolyi in the face. There was a sickening crunch as her nose broke and a weak cry as she sagged in agony back against the young mother, who clutched desperately at her son and shuffled backwards from the violence.

As the man leaned forward to hit Mrs Karolyi again, Alma stepped out from behind the counter.

"Please, leave her," she said. "I'll go with you."

He turned back, his hand still raised with the pickle jar stained with blood. Alma knew she could never look at one of the green containers again without seeing the red specks. He flung the jar carelessly to the floor where it rolled under a display case.

"So be it." He shouted a command to the men and they thrust the five captives through the door, guns trained on the remaining customers.

Alma was the last to be hustled into the van, all of them crammed into the back to sit on the floor, surrounded by the men with guns. As one of the women began sobbing quietly, Alma felt as if her brain was processing the situation on a totally removed level. She could see the tiny details of the scene as if time moved more slowly. A fly buzzed around the head of one man, landing on his ear as he flicked at it. There was a mole on his cheek shaped like the island of Crete, where she had spent one lazy summer. She noticed the broken zip of another man's jacket, the thin material a cheap imitation of an upmarket brand. She saw the broken veins in the outstretched legs of one older woman, her skirt riding up as she tried to stay upright in the lurching van.

As she took in her surroundings, Alma felt the cool aftermath of the adrenalin rush, the sag of exhaustion and a sense that she couldn't fight whatever was going to happen. She thought of her parents at the synagogue and hoped that they were safe, but she felt a sense that she would never see them again. She wanted to rage at the men, appeal to some kind of human decency, but they wouldn't even look at the little group. Was this how people had felt on the way to the camps? Powerless, clinging to a faint hope of reprieve?

The van finally lurched to a halt and the men readied themselves. A panel opened from the front seat and Alma saw the leader's leering face.

"Hungary appreciates your sacrifice," he said, and barked

a command. The doors were thrust open and Alma saw that they were at the banks of the Danube, on the promenade south of the Hungarian Parliament building. She could see the grand lines of the Széchenyi Chain Bridge as they were forced out onto the pavement. Cars drove past on the main road, and a tram pulled up only meters from their position. Concerned faces looked out, but Alma knew that they would do nothing. The more witnesses to a crime, the less likely it was that anyone would act. That was just human nature, it was someone else's problem. Don't get involved, pretend that you didn't see anything, that was the easiest way.

"Take your shoes off," one of the men said, pointing his gun at their feet. "Quickly now."

Then Alma knew what was about to happen and her heart seemed to burst in her chest. She couldn't help a sob escaping her throat as she turned to see exactly where they were. Sixty pairs of shoes cast in iron were lined up in pairs along the banks of the Danube, created as a memorial to the Jews shot by the fascist Arrow Cross militia in World War II. She sank to her knees, sobbing, screaming "Help" at passing cars. But one man pushed her to the ground and another held her down, pulling off her shoes with rough hands. Alma scrambled forward on her knees, thinking that she could escape into the water. The man grabbed her hair and pulled her back and up.

"It's got to be done this way," he whispered. "It is a signal."

Alma felt pain blossom in her back as she heard a sound, a muted gunshot mingled with her own breath and then she was falling forward into the Danube. The freezing water made her gasp but at the same time, she was overheated, her mind fuzzy. She couldn't turn over, she couldn't breathe, she was sinking. In her last moments, she called out to the God of her ancestors for vengeance.

CHAPTER 5

BLENDING INTO THE CROWD of pedestrians, Morgan and Zoltan walked quickly along the boulevard of grand mansions and luxury boutiques in the center of Budapest. They passed the State Opera House, with its tiers of ornate sculpture, but Morgan was too tense to enjoy its beauty.

"Where are we going?" she asked.

"To see an archivist," Zoltan replied, "but his location is less than pleasant. I'm sorry that you have to witness the darker side of Budapest on this trip."

A few minutes later, they arrived at the House of Terror, 60 Andrássy Way, the address feared by Hungarians as the headquarters first of the Fascist Arrow Cross Party and then the ÁVH, the Communist Secret Police. A metal awning over the side of the top story had the word TERROR cut into it with the communist star, so that the sky could only be seen through the lettering. It was now a museum and Morgan thought it brave to acknowledge history with such a statement of fact. For even after the Fascist regime had ended, those of the Communist era had imprisoned, purged and murdered their own people. It seemed incredible that the terrors of the past had not ended with that generation and that now the rise of the right-wing witnessed it beginning again. It seemed impossible that the atrocities of the past could be repeated, yet here they were, seeking to stop violence from escalating as it had done all these years ago.

Pictures of men and women who had disappeared into the building, never to emerge, were displayed on the outside, haunting images of long-gone loved ones, with candles still burning and fresh flowers left in remembrance. Morgan glanced at the faces as she walked past, the stiff portraits in sepia representing brave individuals who had only wished for democracy. Many of them were taken in the wake of the 1956 revolution, when Hungarians had risen up against the Soviets, pulling down the statue of Stalin. The protestors had been quickly and brutally quashed by the Red Army, who killed 20,000 people in the process, arresting and imprisoning many more.

"Georg is a friend from the Army," Zoltan said. "He works within the museum now, cataloging horrors from the past, but he's also a skilled hacker and he knows the Budapest underground scene."

Zoltan spoke to the museum security official, who waved them through the queue of people waiting to enter the macabre memorial. The main entrance hall led into a wide light well, reminiscent of a prison, with walkways around the levels and doors leading off into various departments. A Soviet tank was parked at the bottom of a wall that stretched three floors to the ceiling, covered in black and white photos of victims who had died here.

Morgan was struck by the grey atmosphere that seemed to suck the light out of the air, giving the space a negative energy. Pictures of myriad faces on the walls communicated hopelessness and a complete lack of power, mugshots with obscured features, the shapes in lines of dark black. These people didn't look like the archetypes of revolution. A dumpy woman in a floral print dress. A boy with fine bone structure. A proud businessman in a suit.

As she examined them, Morgan found the features

running together, until the lines of human faces became a repeating pattern on a wall of the past, de-individuation even in death. What must it have been like to be brought here, she thought, knowing that you would never leave?

"Come," Zoltan said, walking through the main gallery towards the shop and administration area. He put his hand gently on Morgan's arm, guiding her away from the vast display of the dead. "We must focus on the present, not the past."

They entered an office suite behind the gift shop, its ceilings low and oppressive. The employees worked on the paperwork of a functioning museum these days, but these rooms had once processed the bureaucracy of intimidation and death. A tall, pale man stood to greet Zoltan, his pallid skin emphasized by his completely black clothing. His features were fine, his eyes a pale brown and Morgan noticed that he wore kohl around them, highlighting the lines in a subtle manner. She could imagine him in more bold makeup, a Goth by night, perhaps, and an academic by day. Morgan found herself intrigued by this man already.

Zoltan spoke a few words in Hungarian, while Georg's eyes rested on her with a questioning gaze. Morgan met his eyes. After a moment, Georg nodded and Zoltan beckoned her forward.

Georg extended his hand and Morgan shook it. His hand was cold and firm, testing her grip as if somehow he could discern through her skin whether she was trustworthy.

"I'm sorry that you couldn't have come at a better time," Georg said, his voice deeper than Morgan had expected, his English slightly accented. "We are fiercely proud of our Hungary, but sometimes she bares her teeth."

"I want to help however I can," Morgan said. Georg nodded and let her hand drop. He looked around at the other workers in the office and nodded to Zoltan.

"Perhaps I can give you a small tour so that you can fully

appreciate this part of our history," he said. "Follow me."

They walked out of the office and down a short corridor, stepping past a line of tourists to claim the next lift. As the doors closed behind them, Georg explained.

"There's another room downstairs that will be more private for our discussions. It's not a nice place to work, the shadows of history are dense down here, but we need privacy for what we seek."

The lift moved slowly down into the depths of the complex. A short video played, featuring an old man who had once cleaned the torture and execution chambers. He described death by garroting, trapping lift occupants into a forceful confrontation with the past. Despite the things she had seen, his matter of fact tone made Morgan feel slightly queasy and claustrophobic as they descended.

"All of this is portrayed as history," Zoltan said. "But many survivors are still alive, and plenty of perpetrators have been left unpunished. The scars of this terror are still raw and the wounds easily reopened." He shook his head. "Sometimes I think that our country is so steeped in blood that the ground has become viscous with it, and one wrong step will suck us all into the maw of the earth."

Georg chuckled. "So poetic, my friend."

Morgan expected Zoltan to be offended at the sarcastic tone, but he merely smiled and shook his head.

"Georg here is a gamer and hacker, and he associates with those who stand for anarchy and revolution."

"What he means is that I know the truth," Georg replied, his kohl-rimmed eyes suddenly serious. "I hack to remain anti-establishment, to keep an eye on those in power and to hold them to account. I don't believe in the innate goodness of mankind, so I seek to ensure that there are balances in place to prevent the rise of such sickness again."

"Why do you work here, then?" Morgan asked. "Surely this place represents everything that you hate?"

Georg nodded. "True, but I would have been one of the first to be thrown to these butchers, just for being different. Every day I confront the bullies of the past and I claim my right to be who I am. As you see, there are still people who want to return to the past, slam people like me and Zoltan into cells and leave us to rot." The lift jerked to a halt. "Come, I will show you why working down here keeps me motivated."

The lift opened into the dungeon of the museum and Morgan followed Georg into the stone corridors as Zoltan trailed behind.

"These are where the prisoners were kept," Georg pointed left and right as they walked indicating where thick doors opened onto cramped cells. Each contained only a dirty wooden pallet and pictures of faces on the walls. Morgan peered into one and saw scratches in the plaster, the marks of desperation an attempt to cling to life for just a little longer. She closed her eyes, the echoes of torture reverberating in her mind. For a moment she felt utterly bereft, with a realization that humanity had always tortured and murdered and always would. Was there was no stopping that darkness, despite how many fought against it?

She clutched at the wall.

"Are you alright?" Zoltan's hand was on her elbow. Morgan opened her eyes to look into his concerned face. Behind him she saw Georg watching her, and she knew that he understood. These men stood against the dark, and she would stand with them. ARKANE usually fought in the realms at the edge of the supernatural, but the violence in Budapest was altogether human.

Morgan nodded. "I'm fine. Let's continue."

"It's just a little further," Georg said, turning and walking deeper into the dungeon labyrinth. "I find it best to work in places that others prefer to avoid."

As she followed, Morgan paused again to look into a

stark stone room. Although the ceiling was low, there was still space for a tall wooden pole with a few steps leading up to it on either side. A simple rope noose hung there, its knot silhouetted on the wood by the bare bulb that lit the pale space. The cell was made somehow more obscene by its emptiness and Morgan felt that the air still held imprints of the murders carried out there. For it was certainly murder, even though it had been justified by a government as a fitting punishment for enemies of the state.

Georg unlocked a door at the end of the long corridor and the three of them squeezed into another cell, barely big enough for a desk and a couple of chairs. On the desk sat a huge, clunky computer from the 1980s.

"It doesn't look like much," Georg said with a cheeky smile. "But this is Budapest hacker central. Now let's take a look at these right-wing lunatics."

He pulled out the chair and sat down at the desk, lifting the old computer to reveal a slim laptop underneath, hidden in plain sight. Georg opened the laptop and his fingers flashed over the keyboard. Morgan was reminded of the ARKANE librarian Martin Klein, whose genius skills were harnessed in the pursuit of esoteric truth. But where Martin was often physically awkward, Georg's presence seemed to intensify as he worked, exuding energy and passion for his quest. Morgan could see that this was a kind of game to him, albeit with serious consequences, a battle of good vs evil in a parallel world where he could work his magic undetected.

"Can you check the chatter on the Eröszak forums?" Zoltan asked. "See if there's any mention of who was involved in the Basilica theft and murder?"

Georg's eyes were fixed on the screen and he didn't reply, just typed faster, his brow furrowing as he read. Morgan could almost see him processing, sifting the information and weighing its importance. The Secret Police would have certainly killed him for being different, she thought, but he would have made a hell of an informant.

Minutes went past before Georg spoke, and Morgan could almost feel Zoltan's impatience beside her. She understood his need for action, it was mostly her own preference, but they needed at least some indication of where to start searching.

Georg's eyes widened and his already pale face blanched.

"What is it?" Zoltan asked.

"There's chatter about a revenge attack," Georg's eyes were hollow, a corridor of time that reflected the massacres of the past. "No specific details but it sounds like a group of Jews have been shot on the banks of the Danube."

Zoltan pushed back his chair with a violent shove, his face contorted, fists tight. His rage seemed to fill the tiny space but just as Morgan thought he would punch the wall, he laid his forehead on the cool plaster and breathed a long exhalation.

"Surely there can be no doubt that this is the work of ultra right-wing nationalists?" Morgan asked, her voice tinged with horror. "Won't the police be investigating this as a matter of urgency?"

"But they're only Jews," Zoltan growled, his voice low. "Just recently, Eröszak supporters marched near a hotel where the World Jewish Congress was meeting. The protestors wore military uniforms, forbidden and outlawed in Hungary, but the police let them march."

Georg nodded.

"Eröszak currently has one third of the Parliament, but across the country the support is much more widespread. And you can see why. Their 'Movement for a Better Hungary' has been embraced as a way to combat unemployment, crime, immigration, and the dependence of welfare cases like the Roma. Jews are again seen as too powerful, a useful scapegoat in a country where we have been murdered and driven out before. These murders will be investigated, but they won't search too hard for those responsible and it won't help us today."

While he spoke, Georg's fingers flashed over the keyboard. "The incident has brought out the big-mouths on the forums. The boasters, the braggers." His face twisted into a sneer. "Idiots." His eyes scanned the pages, while Zoltan still stood against the wall, finally turning to lean against it, his body taut with restrained power. Finally, Georg spun the laptop around for them to look.

"This man was seen in the delicatessen from where they took the victims. He didn't even hide his face, which just shows you the confidence the bastards have."

Morgan and Zoltan leaned closer to the screen. The man was elegant, his features finely chiseled and his nose long and sharp, his black hair slicked into a stylish wave.

"Hollo Berényi, known as the Raven," Georg said. "He's linked to many anti-Semitic attacks as well as to violence against Roma. There's no clear evidence that he's part of Eröszak and, of course, their leader, that slime-ball László Vay, always condemns the violence, but they must be linked somehow. Everything Berényi does furthers the Eröszak cause."

Zoltan grunted. "A few days before the election? Of course it's them. Who else has so much to gain?"

Georg continued. "Some of the chatter indicates that Berényi was also seen around the Basilica early this morning." He clicked another key and more blurred images of the man filled the screen. "Under another name, he spent several years with the Russian Spetsnaz GRU elite military force before disappearing off the radar, surfacing occasionally as a mercenary in various wars. It seems that he offers military strategy for hire, so I think it best to focus on him and what he has been doing."

"Or consider what he might do next?" Morgan said.

Both men looked at her, waiting for more.

"It seems to me that the murder in the Basilica and the theft of the Holy Right has enraged the nation," she continued. "So much so that almost anything would be considered acceptable today, even these murders by the Danube. While the Hand is missing and the Jews blamed, this Berényi can do his worst and be considered a folk hero. From what you've said, I don't think he's finished yet."

"Of course." Georg spun the laptop around again and resumed his tapping. "The police will have to investigate all this, but while there is chaos, they'll just let it ride."

"So if you were going to target Jews in retaliation," Morgan said, "but also escalate the situation by tapping into Hungary's past and attacking symbols of nationalism, what would you do next?"

In the moment's silence that followed, a siren rang out in the building, a deafening 'nee-naw' cacophony. Morgan and Zoltan pressed their hands over their ears while Georg's face froze, as if that sound conjured up a history that he thought lay only in the past.

CHAPTER 6

"It must be just the fire alarm," Georg shouted over the din, "but it can't be a coincidence that you're here." He pressed a key combination and the laptop shut down, encrypting his work. He replaced the ancient machine over the top, then grabbed a small padded case as he indicated the door. "Come on, we must get out of here."

As they ran through the winding corridors of the basement level, Morgan caught glimpses into the rooms they passed. One was stacked with the clothing of those long dead and another filled with crosses illuminated only by candlelight. Eventually the three came to an exit and Georg led them up a tiny staircase. He pushed open the door at the top carefully, inching it open to check the suburban street beyond.

"You must go," he said. "If the police are pulling in people for questioning, you can't be caught or they'll keep you in cells while the Raven rampages out there. I'll go back down to join the evacuation."

"Köszönöm," Zoltan said. "Thank you, my friend."

"Take this," Georg handed Zoltan the padded case. "It's a video camera that will upload via wireless or phone networks to my account. If you can get evidence of what's really going on, I can get it to the press. It's the only way to stop this madness. Words will no longer be enough."

As Zoltan put the camera in his pack, Morgan leaned in and kissed Georg's cheek. "We'll stop this, Georg and it will be thanks to you."

They walked quickly away from the building along Andrassy Boulevard, blending into the crowds who were ogling the scene and snapping photos in their eagerness to be a part of the day's drama. On the other side of the road, Zoltan hailed a taxi, telling the driver to take them towards Buda Castle. As they sped off, a news bulletin came on the radio and the driver turned it up to listen.

***

"Breaking news from the centre of Budapest with reports of violence on the banks of the Danube. Five bodies have been retrieved from the river with gunshot wounds, and the shoes of the victims have been found amongst the iron replica Shoes on the Danube memorial.

An anonymous phone call to the Magyar Hirlap news desk has claimed the murders in retaliation for the theft of the Holy Right, stolen this morning from St Stephen's Basilica, and the brutal murder of Father Zoli Kovács. The anonymous caller threatened further violence until the Holy Right is returned. There are reports of running battles throughout the city as Jewish groups and right-wing nationalists clash. The authorities are struggling to respond to so many concurrent incidents and the police are calling for calm as they proceed with their investigations.

László Vay, leader of the Eröszak party, has just released the following statement.

'Fellow Hungarians, we are all struggling to deal with the terrible theft of the Holy Right, but violence against the people who did this is not the answer. So I ask you for calm today in this beautiful city of ours and let the police do their job.'

Even as László Vay calls for calm, there are reports coming in of a man climbing the Széchenyi Chain Bridge overlooking the Danube. There are no indications of what he's doing up there but we'll bring you updated news as we receive it."

***

The news bulletin finished and the radio segued into a pop song.

"Bastard," Zoltan said. "Vay stokes the fires even with his careful words. I bet whatever's happening on the bridge is down to him as well." He leaned forward to speak to the driver. "Széchenyi Bridge."

The taciturn driver nodded and pulled into another lane.

"Why is the bridge so important?" Morgan asked, her eyes fixed on Zoltan's face, which was creased with worry.

"There are few things that symbolize nationalism for Budapest better than the Széchenyi Bridge," he said. "Designed by an English engineer and opened in 1849, it was the first permanent bridge across the Danube, joining the two halves of Buda and Pest. It was considered an engineering wonder of the world at the time, a symbol of the strength and might of our Empire. In those days, we were kings." Zoltan smiled as if in reminiscence, but then his eyes clouded with shadow. "You know some of Hungary's suffering during the Second World War, but in 1944 we tried to withdraw, even though we were allied with Germany. Hitler wouldn't stand for it and sent German troops here, installing the far-right Arrow Cross party. But Stalin was determined to make an example of Budapest and the Red

Army advanced with over a million men."

Morgan imagined these streets filled with soldiers and frightened people preparing for the impending inevitability of war. Zoltan continued the story.

"With Germans and Hungarians trapped within, Hitler nevertheless declared Budapest a fortress city, to be defended to the last breath of every man. The Siege of Budapest began, just as winter ravaged the city with cold so extreme that the Danube froze."

The taxi was now speeding along by the side of the river, and as they rounded the corner Morgan saw the bridge. Two classical stone arches stood triumphant near the banks and, slung between them, elegant iron suspension cables seemed to hold the structure weightless above the water.

"In January 1945, the Germans couldn't hold the Soviets back and retreated across the river into Buda, destroying all of the bridges as they went, including this one. Only the pillars were left." Zoltan sighed, as if recalling those dark times. "But it didn't stop the destruction. In February 1945 the German and Hungarian forces surrendered. Hundreds of thousands of people were killed or taken to the Soviet labor camps and eighty percent of the city was destroyed or damaged."

Zoltan fell silent and gazed at the bridge as their taxi slowed. Morgan put her hand on his.

"I can see why the bridge means so much," she said. "But I guess it also symbolizes that Budapest can rise again from disaster."

Zoltan nodded. "And if today is about desecrating symbols of nationalism in order to enrage a nation, the bridge is an obvious target."

The taxi pulled to a halt on the Pest side of the bridge and Zoltan paid the driver. Morgan took in the view across the mighty Danube to Castle Hill beyond, the Royal Palace dominating the skyline with its imposing facade. Her eyes dropped to the bridge itself as Zoltan joined her on the side of the main road that ran onto it.

"It's unlikely that this group would expect to destroy the bridge," she said. "They just want something symbolic to blame on the Jewish population and further stoke the fires of unrest."

Zoltan nodded. "I think that they might be saving the finale for the synagogue tonight, and the main aim today is to fire up the mob." He shook his head. "Sometimes there are days when I look to the sky and see only deep blue, a hope of happiness in a world where we have learned to live together in peace. But the storm clouds are never far from this city."

He pointed towards the Parliament building where a swarm of police and media were gathered at the Shoes on the Danube memorial. "We cannot seem to escape the wheel of history that brings violence over and over again."

"But we have today," Morgan said, turning to him. "If we can find the Holy Right, we may be able to stop the escalation. The synagogue would be safe."

Zoltan smiled, his scarred cheek furrowing.

"I'm glad to have you here, Morgan. An outside view helps when the melancholy grows too dark. Come then, let's see what we can find."

Together they began to walk across the bridge as cars accelerated past, their occupants oblivious to the possibility of disaster. Morgan scanned the walkway, her eyes narrowing as she studied each of the people approaching. In Israel, it had been a core part of military training to spot possible bombers and to be vigilant of danger in a new environment. That kind of awareness never leaves you, she thought, even though she had tried to escape that aspect of her past.

Morgan felt the ghost of her father by her side as she walked. Even though he was Sephardi, he had lived amongst Ashkenazi, Jews of Eastern European ancestry, and some of his friends had escaped this very city. Morgan's thoughts flashed to Elian, her husband, who had died in a hail of bullets on the Golan Heights. Defending the community here felt like a tribute to his memory.

As she looked out to the Danube, Morgan saw one of the many open-topped boat tours coming down the river. Tourists leaned out over the water, wrapped in scarves and gloves, but determined to take pictures of the majestic city. Her gaze shifted to the suspension cables, thick and stable, easy enough to scale quickly. Her eyes followed the cable up to where it met the towering classical arch and then widened in surprise. She grabbed Zoltan's arm.

"Look, up there. Is that a man on the top of the arch?"

Zoltan looked up, squinting to see further. Then something moved and they clearly saw a figure crawl across the top of the stone tower.

"What's he doing?" Zoltan said, as the man leaned over the edge, holding something in his hand. Blue spray paint started to etch its way across the stone as the man carefully began his graffiti.

"Oh no," Morgan said. "He's spraying a blue star of David, so whatever happens here next will be blamed on Jews."

"And it's not likely to be just graffiti," Zoltan said, as he swung himself up over the railing and onto the cable. "I'm going up to get him."

Cars began to slow on the bridge as rubberneckers stopped to watch, and Morgan held her breath as Zoltan climbed higher. The man sprayed faster, his lines more shaky as he completed the fourth line. The star was almost finished as Zoltan reached the platform high above the bridge, pulling his body up and holding his arms out to steady himself. Morgan clenched her fists with the tension of watching them as Zoltan rushed the man and threw a punch. The man ducked and then ran to the end of the tower platform. He glanced down towards the Danube, gave a cheeky salute and jumped.

Morgan gasped as the man leapt into space, his legs cycling in the air and then a mini parachute extended from his backpack, slowing his fall. He drifted down onto the boat below as the tourists exclaimed and snapped photos. Morgan saw Zoltan freeze at the top of the arch, looking down at them and then bend to something at his feet. Whatever he had found, she was going after the man who had left it. She clambered onto the ledge of the bridge, assessing the fall to the tourist boat below. She saw the summer awning still hanging above the top deck of the boat. If she could just land on that, it would cushion her fall, but she had only seconds left to decide.

She could see the man from the bridge stripping off his parachute, laughing with the tourists, and posing for photographs, seemingly unconcerned about being identified. The moment slowed in Morgan's mind. Part of her hesitated, a physical brake applied by the ancient lizard brain that protected the body from harm. That part didn't jump from great heights or take physical risks. But then she glanced to her right and saw the people gathered at the Shoes memorial. She imagined the bodies of those murdered earlier that day floating in the freezing river and their echo sixty years ago, a reflection of the atrocities of the past. Morgan thought of the people trapped by the mob in the synagogue, the potential for violence that hung over the city. She jumped.

CHAPTER 7

THE RUSH OF COLD air on her face was bracing as Morgan jumped off the edge of the bridge, looking out to Margaret Island so that she didn't pitch forward as gravity pulled her downward. She knew how to fall from her Krav Maga martial arts experience but also from the years that she had spent rock climbing and canyoning in the hills of Israel. Her muscles remembered the sensation of jumping from the top of waterfalls into icy dark water beneath. She breathed out heavily to try and stem the flood of adrenalin, glancing down to see the canopy of the tourist boat rushing up to meet her. She heard the shouts of the people below, and just before she landed she saw the man turn and spot her. His eyes narrowed and then she lost sight of him as she landed heavily on the canvas.

Morgan felt the air whoosh out of her as she slid towards the deck, turning and grabbing for a hold on the cloth. There was shrieking from the tourists below as she landed with a thump onto the wooden boards, her fall slowed and cushioned by the canopy. It took her a second to reorient herself, and then she heard the revving of a powerful motor. She stood quickly, brushing off the concerned comments of the tourists, pushing through the throng. She hopped up onto the side of the boat and looked towards the source of the noise. At the stern, the man ditched his parachute and was standing, waiting to jump onto a fast-approaching speedboat.

"Hey," Morgan shouted. "Stop him."

But the tourist crowd was more interested in taking photos of this strange incursion than joining in. The man turned at her shout and she saw his hawk-like profile. It was the Raven himself, his mouth twisted into a mocking smile, as Morgan began to fight her way to the back of the boat.

The speedboat pulled alongside, and the Raven leapt deftly in, his step light. Morgan reached the stern just as the boat pulled away, the sound of his laughter just audible above the engine's roar.

***

High above the Danube, Zoltan examined the large package that the man had left. The explosives were encased in clear solid plastic and a prominent timer counted down from five minutes. It was a taunt for anyone who discovered it, for there was no way into the package to stop the bomb going off. Zoltan felt a cold calm descend as he analyzed his options. The bomb wasn't big enough to cause severe damage or destroy the bridge, but it would be a symbolic attack on a nationalist icon, and the media would infer responsibility from the almost complete blue star graffiti. He had to do something, and fast.

The timer ticked into four minutes remaining.

CHAPTER 8

THE SZÉCHENYI SPA BATHS had always been a realm of magic for Elena, a place that transformed her mother from tyrant to soporific princess. During the summers of her childhood, while her mother lay relaxing in one of the hot pools, Elena would play in the shallows, her mind weaving stories of bath nymphs and fairies. She would sink under the water, eyes open, gazing at the hazy figures beneath. Legs loomed like sea monsters and the giants of legend while she fought battles, waiting for the reward from the Bath King who would let her sink down into the blue forever. These moments helped her to forget the packages passed in the changing rooms, and how her mother would duck into the toilets afterwards, her daughter forgotten. She would emerge smiling, rubbing her nose, her body riper somehow.

As Elena walked into the baths today, her body heavy with the false pregnancy stomach she wore, she thought back to those times and how so much had changed. The fairytale of earlier days had been but a dream before the nightmare of her real life had begun. But today, she hoped to escape.

As a child she had discovered that the goodwill from the baths only ever lasted for a short time and then Elena found herself backhanded into silence as she tried to tell her mother of the nymphs. After a while, she didn't mention them anymore. When her breasts had begun to show just before her thirteenth birthday, it was her mother who noticed first.

"Come, Elena," she had said. "We're going shopping."

Elena remembered how excited she had been, for her clothes had been the subject of ridicule at school, hand-me-downs that ill suited her. Now it seemed that her mother would dress her like one of the popular girls. Elena had been confused when the only shop they had entered sold swim-wear and her mother had picked out a tiny bikini. Elena was embarrassed but her mother just adjusted it around her newly formed curves and whispered, "Good, you'll do just fine."

On the next trip to the baths, her mother had kept a tight grip on her hand, making sure that Elena changed into the bikini. In the changing cubicle, her mother had clutched her arm tight, fingernails digging into her arm.

"Now, Elena," she had whispered, her eyes dull. "We need money and you have to earn it. You'll go with someone today and you'll do whatever they want. Don't make a sound or you won't be coming home with me. But be a good girl and there will be money for nice things."

Elena had felt confused, but she would do anything to avoid the beatings her mother doled out. So when the attendant lady had come to fetch her, she had walked behind carefully, following her to the door of one of the private spa rooms.

"I'll get you in thirty minutes," the woman said, her eyes flicking over Elena, dismissing her with one glance. "Go in, then." She pushed open the door and shooed the girl inside the darkened space.

Elena barely remembered what had happened that first time, she had been so terrified. But by the end, her new bikini lay discarded on the floor and her insides felt bruised. The baths had always been a place to get clean, so why did she now feel so dirty?

After the third time, Elena had spoken up, telling her mother she wouldn't go again, that she wouldn't let the men do what they did, that she would scream and tell the police. Her mother had twisted her arm in a Chinese burn, making her listen as she told her daughter that she was a whore, she was ruined and she was nothing. This was her only life choice, this or be sold to the sex trade, and even that would be too good for a little bitch like her. Elena still wondered why her mother hated her so much.

Then, one day, she had entered the spa room and there was a new man in there, his hair a gleaming black. He had wrapped her in a towel and said he only wanted to talk, that he would pay the same amount but he just wanted to speak with her. As he had asked about her school and what she enjoyed doing, Elena had been surprised, but after a few sessions, she began to trust the man and to look forward to time with him. Her mother was none the wiser. A few weeks ago, he had asked her if she wanted to escape the life she led, that if she did one thing for him, he would get her out. She would have money to leave Budapest, to change her life. Did she want that?

Elena wanted that very much, which was why now, nearing her sixteenth birthday, she found herself wearing a false pregnancy stomach, heading into the baths for an antenatal pool session. Earlier, she had gone to an address the man had provided and listened as he told her what to do. "You must wait, stay with the package until it's collected," he had told her. He had made up her face, giving her a wig so that no one would recognize her. It was kind of exciting, like the movies and Elena wanted to do a good job for him. As she left, he had kissed her forehead and she had felt his love. Perhaps he would look after her, rescue her like she had wished the King of the Baths would do in her childhood fairytale.

Wrapping her hands around the pendulous belly, Elena leaned back and looked up at the grand Neo-Baroque entrance. Its pillars and domes were so familiar and yet today, it was as if she saw them with new eyes. The daily stream of visitors was heading through the gates, into one of the largest spa complexes in Europe, with eighteen pools and myriad saunas, steam chambers and corners to relax in. She went through the ritual of entry, her feet following a well-trodden path. The mustard yellow walls dripped with condensation from the steam that billowed through the changing area and Elena felt sweat pool beneath the false stomach. She wondered again what was inside it, knowing not to ask, only hoping that its delivery would secure her freedom.

Inside the baths, she went to her locker and then to the spa room where she had met the man, right next to the pool where the antenatal class was starting. Elena shrugged off the false stomach and placed it beside her on the bench. It looked like a grotesque sack of flesh. Would it hurt to have a look inside it?

She heard the chimes of the clock as her hand reached for the zipper on the side. Elena heard a click and there was a flash of light, a burst of pain and she thought no more as the bomb exploded her young body into a million pieces.

CHAPTER 9

AWARE OF THE SECONDS ticking away, Zoltan peered down at the cars streaming over the bridge and assessed the danger from falling masonry. He looked further out at the boats on the Danube, suddenly noticing that Morgan was now on one of the tourist barges, staring out after a motorboat that was speeding away. He didn't know how she had got down so fast, but he half smiled. She certainly knew how to look after herself, and it was damn attractive.

He glanced down again, feeling a little vertigo. The Danube seemed the only option, for the package wasn't held in place on the bridge. Zoltan picked it up, as gently as he might a precious child, careful not to dislodge any parts. He walked slowly, barely breathing, to the side of the arched tower. Looking down, he inched his way closer to the edge. His heart thumped in fear, for he didn't know the power of the bomb, only sure it would be better off at the bottom of the Danube.

Peering over, he saw a gap in the boat traffic on the river. With a gasp of effort, he threw the package out and away from the bridge. It turned end over end in the air and Zoltan flinched, his muscles tight, expecting an explosion. But the package plopped into the river, floating for a moment and then sinking as the water leaked into the casing. Zoltan looked at his watch, reckoning that there would be just over two minutes remaining.

He stood for a moment looking out over the city, his anger welling up, for he would defend this country he loved to the death. He was a Jew but he was also Hungarian, like he was a son and a brother. A man could be many things, and one aspect did not define him. He would not deny any part of himself to conform to some crazy definition of who was considered a 'real' Hungarian. So he would fight those who tried to divide this glorious city. Zoltan clenched his fists as the time ticked into its final seconds and then he waited, holding his breath.

But nothing came, only the bellowing horns of the boats below, and the hum of the traffic across the bridge. Zoltan exhaled in a long rush as the seconds continued to tick by. He watched the boat that Morgan was on dock at the Vigadó tér pier and turned, heading for the pylon and the tricky climb down. He felt relief flood his body that they had managed to stop at least one of the plans laid for this chaotic day.

Just as Zoltan started his descent, he heard a muffled explosion. His head jerked towards where he had thrown the bomb, but there was nothing there. No plume of water, no ruined boats. The sound had come from the East and he looked in that direction, suddenly seeing a plume of smoke rising above the skyline as the police sirens began to sound.

***

A short distance down Vigadó tér, Zoltan could see the final passengers emerging from the tourist boat. He ran hard towards the pier, pounding the street like he wanted to thump the terrorists who had set off the bomb. Had the bridge just been a decoy? Or was it meant to be a symbolic attack, drawing attention while innocents were targeted at the same time? Zoltan felt a surge of frustrated anger that he channeled into a burst of speed. How dare these people attack his country, his culture, which had already suffered so much?

He slowed on the approach to the ferry pier and stood getting his breath back, waiting for Morgan to disembark. Tourists gabbled away in various languages, some pointing to the plume of smoke evident in the sky to the East. Some were taking photos with a frisson of excitement at being so close to something significant, as if they were somehow immune to the vagaries of attack. Zoltan shook his head, for they didn't realize how arbitrary terror had now become. They should be thanking God that it wasn't their city at the mercy of madmen.

Morgan walked briskly up the metal walkway, having finally extricated herself from the interrogation of the boat's captain. Her face was serious, her eyes fixed on the dark smoky clouds blooming in the sky. As she drew closer, Zoltan noticed the slash of violet in her right eye, almost a burn across the cobalt blue. Her dark curls were tied back and she moved with economy, the grace of a woman who knew how to fight, and how to dance. Who was she really, Zoltan wondered. He had heard of ARKANE, the name mentioned in a whisper when the Jewish elders met to discuss evacuation plans. He knew that the group had an academic side, well represented at conferences, but it was this secret militant arena that he was interested in. Because Dr Morgan Sierra was clearly not just an academic. He hadn't seen her jump, but he didn't know if he could have done the same thing.

"It was the Raven, and the bastard got away," Morgan said, as she joined Zoltan at street level. "I'm sorry."

Zoltan shook his head, dismissing her concern.

"You jumped from the bridge to go after him. I don't think anyone could fault your dedication. What were you thinking?"

Morgan gazed back towards the water.

"I thought I saw the bodies in the Danube, floating there in the water, calling for justice. Those who died today, as well as the ones from seventy years ago." She paused, looking into the eddies of the fast-flowing river. "Did you find anything up there on the arch?"

"There was a bomb, but I threw it in the Danube before it timed out. It was encased in plastic, tamper-proof." He gestured upwards to the smoke dissipating in the sky above. "But seeing that, I suspect it was a decoy anyway."

Morgan nodded.

"They were playing the local news on the boat. The bomb was at the Széchenyi Baths. Twelve dead." She paused. "It was during an antenatal class, so there were pregnant women amongst the casualties."

Zoltan clenched his fists, willing his rage to a simmer, but there was nothing he could do to help those people now. He and Morgan had to focus on what must surely come next.

"There was an anonymous call to the TV station," continued Morgan. "The bombing has been claimed by a previously unknown Jewish group, in retribution for the Danube murders."

Zoltan snorted, shaking his head. "As if it could have been organized so quickly. They've set this up so well. Whoever is behind this must have been planning it for months."

"That guy from Eröszak is calling on the government to boycott Jewish businesses until the perpetrators are brought to justice. Of course, he's not advocating violence officially but his supporters are calling for a march tonight, in solidarity with the victims." Morgan put her hand on Zoltan's arm, her voice urgent. "We need to find the Holy Right, it's the only way to stop a bloodbath after dark."

Zoltan gazed across the water at the Palace, a dominant presence that loomed above the city. On the edge of the battlements, he could just make out the giant statue of the

Turul, the divine messenger bird of Magyar origin. In the myths of the beginning, it had perched on the top of the Tree of Life, along with the spirits of unborn children in the shape of birds. It was a symbol of power, strength and nobility, a bird of prey with a beak that could rip the hearts from the chests of men, sacrificed on its blood-spattered altar.

As he considered the symbol, trying to discern a pattern in the chaos, Zoltan thought about Castle Hill itself. It was the centre of the nation, a symbol of the might of Hungary as it had once been and how some wanted it to be again. While Pest was the realm of the past, the Ghetto, the Basilica and a Parliament that had become too left wing for many, Buda was the proud fortress of might, the dominion of the future. Surely a nationalist cause would want that symbol to be at the heart of their strategy, and something niggled at the back of Zoltan's mind about the tunnels beneath the hill.

He took out his mobile and dialed Georg, who answered quickly.

"I need you to go back on the right-wing chat boards," Zoltan said. "Can you see what you can find from 2011?"

While he waited for Georg to search, Zoltan turned back to Morgan.

"There's an ancient labyrinth beneath Castle Hill. It was shut down a few years ago under suspicious circumstances, around the time when Eröszak was on the rise."

His attention returned to the phone. "Great, we'll check it out."

Zoltan pointed to Castle Hill. "Let's head up there, it's the only lead I can think of right now."

He led the way up the wide boulevard away from the ferry port. Stopping in front of a giant billboard advertising the elections, Zoltan looked up into the face of László Vay. His scar contorted as his mouth twisted with anger.

"This man knows nothing of honor, and he will do anything to further his pursuit of power. None of what has happened today is beyond him, for he wants to win this election, and I think he aims to waltz in on the back of a nationalist uprising. I knew him once, you know, we were friends ... but then one day I discovered the true man behind that perfect smile."

As Zoltan spoke, he remembered that dark day in Bosnia, when his friendship with Vay was obliterated.

***

Srebenica, Bosnia and Herzegovina. Spring 1995.

"Come on, Zol. Seriously, you're always so slow. You can't do anything for it now, let's just leave."

Zoltan didn't look up from the body he was examining, this one just a boy with a gunshot through his forehead. He was used to the taunts of his friend, the dismissive attitude to the people they were there to protect. The child's arms were curled around himself as if he had tried to find comfort in the moments before death. Zoltan found himself silently reciting the opening words of the Kaddish, the Jewish prayers for the dead, even though the boy was probably Muslim in this part of town. Finally he rose.

László was smoking a cigarette, his body relaxed. He lifted his face to the sun, caught in a brief sunbeam, and reveled in its warmth. There were no dark shadows under his indigo eyes, only the movie star looks that made him the envy of the other soldiers. Zoltan didn't know how László managed to shrug off the deadening weight of sadness that he found engulfed him every day.

They both worked as part of the peacekeeping force, seconded from the Magyar Honvédség, the Hungarian army, to help the Dutch United Nations team. But Zoltan knew that there was no way of keeping the brittle peace for long and he felt the palpable tension in the air. These people hated each other and there had always been violence in this region. It was a tribal place, united only by the fake lines drawn on maps that were as fragile as the paper they were inked on. Thousands of Christian Serbs, Jews and Gypsies had been sent to camps from here under the Nazis and after the war, Yugoslavia had been created. Now, it had broken down, as Muslim nationalists demanded a centralized independent Bosnia, Serbian nationalists wanted to stay near Belgrade-dominated Yugoslavia, and Croats wanted an independent Croatian state.

"Do you even give a shit about this place, Laz?" Zoltan asked as he stole the cigarette from his friend's fingers.

"Of course not," László said. "This land should be ours anyway. After all, Bosnia-Herzegovina was part of the Austro-Hungarian Empire a hundred years ago. Maybe if they all kill each other, it will be ours again."

Seeing the fanatical look in László's eyes, Zoltan sighed and shook his head. His friend had always been an extreme patriot, harking back to the old days of Hungarian glory. They had been the best of friends once, when their fathers had been business partners in a chain of Jewish shops in Budapest and they had played war games amongst the sacks of goods while the adults talked and drank together. László's mother wasn't Jewish, which technically meant that he wasn't either, but that hadn't been important to the boys back then.

A rattle of bullets startled the men and they flattened themselves against a wall. This area was known to be raided by Serb incursions and the sound had been close. Behind a nearby fence, Zoltan could hear the harsh laughter of a group of men, and then a woman's cry. He instinctively raised his gun and stepped forward quietly. László reached out to hold his arm.

"Don't," he said quietly. "It's not your fight."

"Then what the fuck are we doing here?" Zoltan whispered, his rage rising at the impotence of the peacekeepers to stop any kind of violence. It didn't matter to him which group was inflicting the pain, only that the suffering of the innocents would stop. This dirty war was marked by systematic rape as a weapon, mainly by the Serbs against the Bosniaks. Zoltan had heard them boasting of the 'little Chetniks' they would leave behind in the wake of abused women.

The woman screamed again, but the noise was cut short by shouting voices and the sound of a fist slamming into flesh. Zoltan pulled his arm away from László, stepping forward through the rubble of the streets to peer around the edge of the fence. There were six men, wearing the uniform of Serb nationalists, surrounding a woman who was sprawled, weeping, across the body of a dead man. One of the men said something, nodding at the woman and began to unbuckle his belt.

Zoltan felt his heart beating hard in his chest. In some way, this tiny scene represented a microcosm of this conflict, and of every injustice against the vulnerable. Zoltan had heard the stories of Budapest under the fascists, then the Communists, how friends had given each other up in exchange for another day of freedom. He couldn't alter his own country's past, but perhaps he could change this woman's future.

He stepped out from behind the fence, his gun relaxed by his side. Knowing that he and László were outnumbered, it would be better to reason with them.

"You're a long way from your camp, guys," Zoltan said as the men swung round to look at him. Their faces were hostile, and they raised their guns as they formed a phalanx around the woman, claiming their prize. Her sobs filled the air before one of the men spoke, his English halting.

"You … go. This," he gestured at the woman. "Ours."

Zoltan stepped forward, his left hand outstretched in a

gesture of placation. His heart was hammering, but he knew that if he walked away now, the woman would be brutally violated. He still had a chance to stop it.

"This woman is under UN protection," he said. "So I think you had better leave."

One of the group laughed and turned away, saying a few words and reaching down to pull the woman off the body of her husband by her hair. She screamed again. Zoltan raised his gun and immediately, the other men had their weapons readied. Zoltan's senses were heightened, the metallic smell of weapons overlaid with the stink of the soldiers' sweat thick in his nostrils.

He felt rather than heard László emerge from behind. A surge of gratitude washed over him at his friend's belated backup. But then he heard a click near his ear, and realized that Laszlo's gun was pointed at his own head. A flush of betrayal rocked him.

"We're sorry for the intrusion," László said, his voice smooth, as if they were at a gentlemen's club, not on the broken streets of Srebenica. "My friend here was just leaving."

The Serbs laughed and lowered their weapons. Zoltan felt László pulling him backwards as the six men turned to their prize, two men of them now unbuckling their pants, as the woman wept at their feet.

Zoltan felt as if the world slowed in that moment, his brain frantically searching for a solution. His eyes fell on a pile of weaponry that the Serbs had left discarded to one side.

A grenade. It was the only way.

He felt almost manic, desperate to get to the woman and stop the soldiers. László wouldn't shoot him, he knew that, but he also knew that his friend would always choose the easy way out. There would be no back up.

The Serbs had their backs turned and as two men held

the woman down, another bent to pull off her lower garments as she sobbed in desperation.

"Just walk away, Zol. You can't help her." László's voice was honey, tempting him with the easy path, but the words of Simon Wiesenthal, the persecutor of Nazi criminals, echoed in Zoltan's mind. *For evil to flourish, it only requires good men to do nothing.*

Zoltan broke away from László's grip, running for the pile of weaponry, his eyes fixed on a grenade. He heard swearing and then a gunshot but didn't flinch, steeling his body and flinging himself down behind the pile as he grabbed a grenade from the top. Looking back briefly, he could see Laz ducking back behind the wall, his face turned away. Zoltan knew that he had mere seconds before the men advanced to kill him, so he pulled the pin from the grenade and launched it, throwing it far enough away that it would explode against a nearby building.

The soldiers shouted and ducked as the grenade landed and then exploded, raining debris down from the scarred and shattered tenement block. They turned towards the weapons pile just as Zoltan pulled the pin and lobbed another grenade. This time the soldiers scattered, firing behind themselves at him and the weapons pile. The last soldier pointed a gun at the woman's head as he turned away. Zoltan leapt from his hiding place and charged the man as the gun went off. His eyes had flicked up at the movement so the bullet just missed the woman's head as she curled into a fetal position.

An explosion rocked the little square and as masonry began to fall, Zoltan threw his body over the woman, trying to protect her from the rain of hell. As the other soldiers ran from the scene, he felt a slicing pain in his cheek and a burning on the side of his face as he lay there, hoping that he could just save this one innocent.

***

Zoltan touched the scars on his cheek as he looked up into László's face on the billboard, remembering that day. After the incident, their friendship had finally ruptured and split. László had inveigled himself into an officer's position, allying himself with nationalist interests and eventually pursuing a political career. He was the embodiment of what most would consider success, becoming wealthy and influential in the public arena. Zoltan had followed his moral compass, giving up the pursuit of power to stand up for those who could not defend themselves.

He felt a light touch on his arm, and turned to see Morgan's face, a question in her eyes. Zoltan knew that he could trust her, their fast friendship built on a shared belief in humanity that men like László would never understand or honor.

"Sorry," he said, glancing at his watch. "Let's go. The march will start early and as dusk falls, I fear that evil will stalk this city again."

CHAPTER 10

WHEN THEY REACHED THE tourist-ridden precinct of Castle Hill, Zoltan led Morgan away from the throng down a dogleg alleyway.

"There's an old entrance for the labyrinth workers back here," he said. "Tourists used the official gateway but that's been closed since 2011."

"Why did they shut it down?" Morgan asked.

Zoltan shrugged. "There are many conspiracy theories, because it was stormed by the police and the Inspectorate for the Environment one July day. The tourists and workers inside just had to leave, with no reason given. Some say that the company running the place didn't have the right permits, but others hint at something darker here, criminal activity or the occult. From what Georg found in the chat rooms, this could well be a secret Eröszak meeting place." He stopped in front of a nondescript wooden door. "This is it."

Pulling the tire iron from his bag, Zoltan levered the door open, cracking the lock mechanism as it splintered in the frame. A metal staircase led down into the earth, and already Morgan could feel cool air flowing up from below. Pulling torches from the pack, they trod lightly, but their footsteps still made a soft clang as they descended into the dark.

At the bottom, a tunnel carved from the rock stretched into the heart of the hill. They stood silently for a moment, the sound of dripping permeating the damp atmosphere. Water welling from the depths of the earth under Budapest had brought with it healing properties, feeding the rejuvenating hot spring spas, and over millennia, the waters had also carved out a complex of subterranean tunnels and caves. Now Zoltan and Morgan followed one of these tunnels into the labyrinth, and in the chill air, it felt as deserted as it would have been when it was created.

They walked quietly, listening for any hint of what might lie before them. Morgan reached out a finger to touch the cool wall of stone, remembering the catacombs of Paris where she had run from Milan Noble's men. But those corridors were walls of bone arranged in tribute to the millions of plague dead, whereas this place was ancient, perhaps already here when humanity was born. It would still be here when the span of human existence ended, when the wars exhausted themselves and the earth could rest again.

"The company that ran this place created a bizarre tourist trail in the labyrinth," Zoltan said, his voice low. "It was meant to be a journey into the history of Budapest and also a kind of spiral path into the self."

"I can see the attraction of the symbolism." Morgan whispered back. "In Jungian psychology, the labyrinth is a powerful symbol of the unconscious. We protect our secrets even from ourselves by winding them in deep, hidden mazes. In myth, the labyrinth held the Minotaur, the beast we must all slay to reconcile our true selves."

Zoltan grunted softly. "Enough of stories. There may be real beasts down here."

Their torch beams flickered around the tunnels running off to the side. A shadow of a figure loomed suddenly from the dark, and Morgan started suddenly, her hand moving instinctively to where she would normally carry a weapon,

"It's OK," Zoltan reassured her. "It's just one of the statues they have down here, called the Guides of the Soul. The weird red figures are everywhere. It's an odd place, with different galleries according to the time period and even a cafe, deserted now of course, which makes it perfect for a ready-made bunker in the heart of the city."

They continued down a long corridor with carved stone heads atop life-size pillars on either side, their faces featureless, similar to the giant statues of Easter Island.

"This is known as the Axis of the Earth," Zoltan said. "People would come alone to spend the night here, considering their lives."

They rounded another corner into a cavernous room, the stone walls bare of decoration. Dominating the room was a stone pillar carved with two faces, one leonine and the other like some mythical dark elk.

"This is the double faced shaman, the táltos," Zoltan whispered, and Morgan heard a touch of reverence in his tone. "The ancient Hungarians believed in soul dualism, a bodily soul for this physical realm, and another that roamed free in the world. The shaman had a watcher spirit that guarded his physical body as his powerful soul traveled."

Morgan played the torch over the figure, dual faces with harsh lines, a powerful embodiment of the shaman, while leaves and branches curled down the pillar. Zoltan saw the movement of her light and explained.

"The tree of life connects the worlds of Magyar myth, the upper home of the gods, this middle world where we dwell and the underworld entwined in its roots, where Ördög dwells, creator of all evil."

Morgan felt her skin crawl at the pronunciation of the name of the Hungarian devil, for in Zoltan's mouth, the myth seemed to live, and they were down in his dark realm now. There was a palpable sense of menace, as if the walls themselves exhaled a poison. She almost expected to see dark shapes oozing from the stone, shapes that demanded another soul to gorge on.

"The souls of the táltos could travel between the realms, drenching the ghosts and interceding for humanity with the gods, some say preventing the destruction of all by the ravaging of demons." Zoltan paused, running his fingers down one branch of the tree. "But their strength has disappeared along with the people's faith in them. And where were they in the dark days of the ghetto?" he murmured.

Rounding a corner, Morgan saw a massive head emerging from the earth, his crown a grotesque bulk that pushed out of the ground. It was a giant buried by the mountain, a fallen king, perhaps representing the fall of Austro-Hungary, Morgan thought, a once-mighty empire that struggled to rise from the dirt of history. In her mind, she saw the figure shake itself free to rule again. At first he would be noble and just, dealing fairly with his faithful subjects. But this king had twisted plans, and soon after he emerged, he would bring his giant club down upon the people.

Zoltan stopped suddenly, putting his hand on Morgan's arm, his fingers clutching it with a tight grip. He flicked his torch off and she followed suit. They stood in the dark, barely breathing. Then Morgan heard it too, a pair of voices raised in argument ahead of them. Zoltan slipped off the backpack and pulled out the camera case Georg had given them. Carefully, he inched the zipper down and freed the device, pressing a button so that a tiny red light glowed in the dark.

Morgan felt the cool stone on her back, her breath ragged in the air. She strained to hear the words, but they were muffled in the angular acoustics of the cave, deadened by the tons of stone above them. She felt Zoltan squeeze her arm and pull her forward, moving his hand down to hers so that they could inch along the wall together towards the sound.

There was light up ahead, the warm glow of candles. As they paused at a bend, hidden in the shadows, Morgan could see two figures, hands raised as they argued with each other. A warped stone cross with stumped ancient limbs stood at the end of the corridor and the walls were flanked with stone pillars topped with spiked metal roundels. It seemed like an altar to a pagan hybrid of Christianity and the ancient Magyar faith.

The voices were clearer now, an argument in fast Hungarian and a sub-text of gesticulation. One man grabbed at the other and his face angled towards the candlelight. With the sharp nose and shining black hair, Morgan recognized Hollo Berényi, the Raven, the man she had chased from the bridge. She felt Zoltan tense beside her, bracing himself for action, but they had no weapons and a frontal assault up this thin corridor would be suicidal. Recording the encounter would be far more valuable for their cause and Zoltan silently held up the camera, his hand obscuring the red light.

"They're arguing about when to reveal the relic," Zoltan whispered by her ear. "Berényi wants to take it to the rally, claiming that it will escalate the violence tonight if they announce its recovery from the Jews who stole it. He wants to leave now, but the other man talks of using it for some kind of ceremony first."

A third man stepped from the shadows behind the altar, his voice halting the argument with authority. Morgan recognized László Vay from the political posters and felt Zoltan draw in a sharp breath at seeing his former friend in this dark place.

Berényi seemed placated by the words, shrugging as László spoke, but clearly uncomfortable with losing the argument. He made a final comment, then spun on his heel and stalked away down a tunnel away from the altar cavern.

"He's going ahead to make sure everything is ready at the rally," Zoltan whispered, and in his words, Morgan could hear his indecision as to whether to go after the man. Berényi was the blunt instrument of neo-nationalist wrath, a Turul with hooked claws and a beak that could disembowel its victims, a mythical creature of violence and blood. He had to be stopped, but they both knew that László Vay was the more dangerous in the long run.

László placed something reverently on the ancient altar, wrapped in a white cloth. Zoltan was transfixed by the object and he raised the camera again. Morgan dared to hope that it would capture the detail of the scene in the semi-darkness.

The other man started to chant, his hands raised to heaven in supplication as he moved behind the altar. The intonation was strange: not just the words but even the rhythm of his prayers was off-beat somehow. The words rolled through the caves, echoing in the long corridor, as if he was calling the ancient spirits to bear witness. In the flickering candlelight, Morgan suddenly saw his face, tattooed with intricate patterns of leaves that seemed to morph into demonic visages as his mouth twisted with entreaties to the spirit world. She saw that he had missing teeth and those remaining had been blackened and sharpened, like a maw of Hell. This man made her flesh crawl, and Morgan itched for a gun.

"Those are Magyar ritual prayers," Zoltan whispered. "He's a táltos, a shaman." Morgan heard the undertone of shock in his voice. "I've heard of this tattooed man. He channels dark magic back to this country, allying himself with the Far Right who can give him the blood sacrifice he needs."

László leaned forward and, with reverence, unfolded the cloth, as the prayers of the táltos grew more frenzied. Inside was a brown, leathery object that reflected the candlelight in dull hues, its patina like a horse chestnut at the end of autumn. It was the size of a clenched fist, and in that second, Morgan realized that it was the Holy Right Hand of St Stephen.

László fell to his knees in front of the altar, like a king waiting to be anointed. He sang out resonant words, pausing as the táltos echoed each phrase.

"He claims the Right as his own," Zoltan whispered. "He claims Hungary as a new Empire under his rule. He entreats the Gods to accept the blood sacrifice offered today in their name."

As the táltos chanted louder, he picked the relic up with both hands and began to wave it in a figure of eight in the air, the symbol of eternity. Morgan could see that László's eyes were shining with fanaticism as he watched it circle, as if this Hand bestowed on him the right to rule. The táltos touched László's face with it, stroking the living flesh with the thousand year old relic in a grotesque blessing. A shudder ran through László, but Morgan could see that it was ecstasy, not revulsion, that shook him.

Placing the Hand back on the altar, the táltos took up a ceremonial knife. Strange symbols were carved on the handle, evoking the myths of the Magyar war gods. With his chants growing more guttural and violent, the táltos cut a sliver of flesh from the mummified hand. He placed the slice into a chalice and filled it with dark liquid from a flask, swirling it around as he intoned ancient words.

László opened his mouth for the tainted host, closing his eyes in prayer as the táltos tipped the chalice.

CHAPTER 11

MORGAN WATCHED LÁSZLÓ SWALLOW, chewing a little on the long dead flesh, and she felt a rush of nausea at his cannibalism. The camera light still glowed under Zoltan's hand, and she realized that this footage would show the politician as a madman. Where people would tolerate racist violence, bigotry and hatred, they would not accept superstition and desecration. Eröszak was standing for economic revival in a greater Hungarian Empire, not the resurrection of myth and dictatorship.

"Enough," Zoltan whispered, pressing a button on the camera. They slipped back around the corner and he handed it to Morgan. "You need to get this out of here so that it can transmit above ground to Georg. It's the evidence we need to stop the rally. I'll deal with these two and then I'll bring out the relic."

The look in Zoltan's eyes was that of a man defending his family from invasion. Morgan knew that he wouldn't stop until Hungary was free from these fanatics, when it was a country where all Hungarians could live together, whatever their beliefs. She nodded and touched his hand, leaning in close.

"Be careful," she whispered. "Your people need you alive."

Then on light feet, she ran through the cave, back the way they had come.

***

Zoltan watched Morgan go, sending up a prayer that she would make it in time to stop further escalation. He pulled the tire iron from his pack, rounding the corner as the prayers of the táltos reached a crescendo. László knelt in front of the altar facing the twisted cross. As his mouth opened again to receive the final libation, Zoltan stepped from the shadows, crashing the weapon against one of the metal roundels as he ran towards them. The noise resounded through the cave and the táltos fell silent as both men spun to face the sound.

"No," László bellowed with rage, leaping up, his ritual of power interrupted. His hand fell to his belt for a weapon but as his fingers closed around the butt of a gun, Zoltan was upon him, swinging the tire iron. László rolled away and the blow glanced off his shoulder as Zoltan swung back for another strike. The táltos backed away, his tattooed face showing no fear, only a curiosity at this development. His prayers changed again and Zoltan heard the beginnings of a curse, words that had echoed down the centuries as a harbinger of desperate suffering.

László pulled his gun and turned, firing just as Zoltan slammed the tire iron down on his arm. The shot went wide, ricocheting off the stone walls and the gun fell clattering to the ground. As László clutched at his arm, Zoltan shoved the metal back into his stomach, driving the wind from him as he fell to his knees, coughing. After all the years of politics, the man was soft, relying on others to fight his battles. Zoltan stood over him with the metal bar raised, muscles tense.

"It's finished, Laz. I'm taking the relic back to the Basilica."

László laughed through his wheezing attempts to draw breath, looking up at Zoltan from the ground as he clutched his damaged arm.

"You just don't get it, do you? Always the brawn, never the brains, eh, Zoltan. Even your father knew that I was the better man."

Zoltan gripped the tire iron harder, wanting to slam it down and destroy this man, responsible for so much violence and capable of so much more.

"You can't stop the march of progress," László continued. "This country wants change, it wants the fucking Jews and Roma out. We will finish what Hitler started and the Soviets continued."

Zoltan felt a strange sensation possess him. It was as if he stood at the pivotal point of a chain of history, violence repeating itself throughout generations. He was alone, standing against the tide of hate, but he felt the weight of history buoy him up. The Jews had survived unceasing waves of brutality against them, and he would survive this. To bring the tire iron down and finish László would make him a martyr, killed by a Jew, sparking further cycles of retribution. Zoltan stepped back towards the gun. He needed to get László out of there to face some kind of public reckoning. But then the prayers of the táltos stopped and Zoltan heard the rasp of the gun, and a faint click.

He dived for the shelter of the nearest stone pillar just as the tattooed man fired. Zoltan felt a burning sensation in his arm and heard László laugh as he clutched at the wound, feeling warm blood pulsing out.

"You see, Zoltan, even the Magyar ancestors reject you. But I will be a hero today, wounded in action while killing the Jew who stole the relic and returning it to the people myself." László looked briefly at his watch. "I will produce you at the rally, the perfect scapegoat, a Jew with a personal grudge against me."

Zoltan heard László get up and walk across the cave towards the táltos, knowing that if László got the gun, he was finished. What did he have to lose anymore, he thought, and launched himself back out of the shelter of the rock, hurling himself at his old friend. Zoltan slammed into László, using his bulk to smash his body against the altar and knock them both into the táltos, who dropped the gun in his haste to back away. They ended up on the floor, a tangle of bodies, each scrambling to grab hold of the other, a snarling mass of aggression, reduced from men to beasts.

Zoltan landed a blow to the tattooed nose of the táltos, and blood gushed immediately. Zoltan saw the hatred in his eyes as the man scrabbled away on hands and knees, before standing and running off down the corridor.

His attention momentarily diverted, Zoltan felt László roll out of the grip of his damaged arm and lurch for the tire iron lying close by. He spun quickly and grabbed the man, slamming his head against the hard ground, pinning the searching fingers with a tight grip. László groaned and Zoltan felt his blood lust rise, aware that he had only to carry on smashing the man's head and it would be over. He thought of Srebenica, the moment he had seen the truth of his friend's heart. He slammed once more and then stopped, lying panting against László's prone body, trying to catch his breath. He spotted the gun a little way from them and stood, shaking with the effort.

Zoltan fell to his knees by the gun, wanting to rest now, to lean against the wall and just close his eyes. He reached for the weapon, and as he did so a sound came from behind him, a scream of rage, almost inhuman in its ferocity.

CHAPTER 12

ZOLTAN REACTED QUICKLY, GRABBING the gun and spinning towards the shriek. László held the tire iron high, its arc heading straight for Zoltan's head, his eyes a berserker's, crazed with savagery. There was no choice in that moment and Zoltan fired the gun, almost reflexively, as if he were under fire in enemy territory. It was kill or be killed, and here, under his great city, it had finally come to this most basic of human drives to stay alive.

The bullet hit László in the chest and the look on his face was pure disbelief. He dropped the tire iron and turned, clutching at the altar. The Holy Right still lay there and as he toppled, László grabbed it, pulling it to his chest like a talisman. His blood pumped out, soaking the mummified hand and Zoltan could only watch as his once friend died, his eyes going blank as his spirit joined the ancestors that haunted the cave system.

Zoltan heard footsteps in the stone corridor. He gripped the gun again, aware that there were only a few bullets left. He tried to rise, but was so weakened by the blood loss and the aftershock of the fight that he sank to the floor again. A figure rounded the corner and he saw it was Morgan, her eyes alight with concern. She ran to him.

"I heard the shots," she said. "I had to come back. We have

to finish this together, Zoltan. But first, I need to get you to a hospital." Morgan pressed her hands over the wound in Zoltan's arm, blood oozing out around her fingers. She looked over at László's corpse, with his blood forming a pool around him before the altar. Zoltan clutched at her hand, his eyes searching hers for judgment.

"I didn't mean to kill him, Morgan, but now I have to wonder … Would you have killed Hitler in 1933, given a chance? Before he gained the kind of power that led to the camps? Before Eichmann slaughtered the Jews of Budapest?"

"It's impossible to say." She shook her head. "Of course we would have in hindsight, but no one knew what kind of man Hitler would become in the beginning."

"Or no one would have believed it of him." Zoltan's eyes closed for a moment. "Except his closest friends, perhaps. Those who knew him before he became powerful, when he let down his guard and showed his true lack of empathy. László could have gone that way, Morgan. I know it. He could have even been worse in an age of media devotion to the beautiful, where his perfect face could hide his rotten soul."

"I can't believe that the people of this country would allow genocide again, that Europe could let something like that happen."

Zoltan smiled bitterly, his scar twisting into a grimace. "Srebenica was only 1995, and Rwanda the year before. We let it happen, and history repeats itself because people remain the same underneath. Brutal, tribal, violent."

Morgan shook her head. "Not all of them."

"Enough of them to call for the secret police to create a register of Jews. Enough of them to burn a synagogue with innocents inside if we don't stop that rally," Zoltan said. "Berényi is still out there, stirring up a hornet's nest of neo-nationalist hate. The city is dry kindling waiting for the spark and we have to dampen it."

He struggled to push himself up from the floor, but his face whitened with the effort and he sank back.

"I don't think you'll be much use against Berényi," Morgan said. "I need to get you some help."

"There's no time," Zoltan said, his eyes pleading with her. "You have to stop him without me." He looked round at László's body. "And I need to deal with the body and get far away from here, because if it's discovered that a Jew killed the nation's favorite son, albeit in self-defense, we'll have more than a day of terror." He pulled his cellphone from his pocket. "Call Georg from outside and tell him where I am. He'll be able to find out where the rally is, too." He pushed at her arm weakly. "Now, go."

***

As Morgan ran back through the cave system, she felt a rising sense of fatigue, for despite the death of one man who had incited racial hatred, there were many more ever-ready to take his place. The caverns seemed oppressive, their unyielding walls a reminder that the nature of human-ity doesn't change. But there were furrows in the rock and trickles of water that ran down the walls, carving their way over centuries. Perhaps that was the only way, she thought as she ran, the gentle, insistent push of water reflecting the slow progress of equality. She remembered little Ilona at the synagogue, her eyes wide with terror, fearful of something that she didn't understand and a world where already some hated her for no reason. Enough, Morgan thought, the time for gentle insistence was over.

Emerging through the battered door into the light, Morgan checked the cellphone coverage and finally managed to get a signal. She switched on the camera as she dialed Georg and watched the bars on the screen as the files were transmitted. He answered within two rings.

"Zoltan, are you OK?" he asked, his voice blurred as he covered the mouthpiece to disguise his words.

"It's Morgan," she said quickly. "We've got video footage but Zoltan's hurt. He needs help but it has to be secret. He needs evacuation from the labyrinth under Castle Hill." She heard Georg's shocked intake of breath as she recounted the events.

"We're still outside the Andrassy offices," he said. "Many employees are drifting home so I can slip away too. I know those caves and I'll get Zoltan out of there." Morgan gave him the directions to the back entrance where she stood.

"Do you know a doctor?" she asked. "He needs urgent medical attention but it needs to be discreet."

Georg laughed, a harsh bark. "We're Jews, Morgan. Doctors are something we have a lot of. Don't worry, Zoltan will be fine, and we'll keep him safe. I'll need time to process the video before we can release it to the media. Shall I meet you near the labyrinth entrance?"

Morgan hesitated a moment, a part of her longing to wait for him and then fly home as she had meant to hours ago. But then she thought of the bodies in the Danube, imagining her own father's face amongst the dead. It could have been him, she thought. It could have been Elian, or any of those I love.

"No," she said. "I need to go after Berényi. He's heading for some kind of rally, a gathering of nationalists. If he succeeds in enraging the crowd, there could be a bloodbath before we can get the media to release the video."

"Thank you, Morgan," Georg said, and she heard unspoken layers of meaning in his words. Some were called to fight and others to work behind the scenes, and Georg knew that they were both important today. "Just a minute, I'll check the chatter and call you right back."

He cut the line and Morgan stood for a moment. She didn't want time to think about what she was doing, and she knew Director Marietti would have told her to get out of town hours ago, for this wasn't a fight that ARKANE should be involved in. There were no religious mysteries here, only a deep-rooted hatred embedded in the DNA of the region, startled into life again by economic crisis and spiraling unemployment. But Morgan knew that she couldn't leave knowing she might have prevented violence.

The phone rang, and she answered it quickly. Georg's voice was rushed, and there were street sounds in the background now as he spoke.

"I'm in my car now, heading for the labyrinth. The video is processing and I'm editing it to remove your voice and Zoltan's in the corridor." The sound of horns made Morgan move the phone from her ear, then he continued. "I'm also monitoring the neo-nationalist forums and there's chatter about a large gathering at Memento Park, just outside the city center. One right-wing fundamentalist blogger has been tweeting about the atmosphere building there, how they're waiting for something huge to kick off, how the Jews will pay, that kind of thing."

"Sounds like it might be the place." Morgan said, as she headed back towards the main road of Castle Hill. "What are the police doing? Surely that's got trouble written all over it."

"They're strung out all over the city, trying to quell the unrest evident in a spate of revenge attacks on both sides. The Jewish community isn't entirely innocent in this anymore, Morgan. Some groups are taking steps to retaliate for the Danube murders."

Morgan closed her eyes, willing frustration from her.

"Of course, this escalation is exactly what Eröszak intended. I'll get to the rally and see what I can do."

"There will be a lot of media there on a day like this. With so much potential for conflict, it's a broadcaster's dream and we can use that." Georg paused and Morgan could almost hear his brain whirring. "There's a USB key in the side of the camera, do you see it?"

She turned the camera over in her hands, finding the tiny device embedded in the base.

"Yes, got it."

"If you can plug that into a media device, I can hack in and send the edited video. It will be more effective if you can do it at the rally rather than me posting it on the net."

Morgan thought of the potential danger of walking into a neo-nationalist rally and trying to share the explosive video. It would be hard enough to get that close and even if she could, the crowd wouldn't exactly be receptive to the dark unveiling of their favorite son.

"I'll try," she said. "Keep your phone handy."

She thrust her hand out, waving at an oncoming taxi.

CHAPTER 13

THE TAXI DROPPED MORGAN a little way from the entrance to Memento Park because the roads were so busy. It seemed that all of Budapest was gathering, or at least those who supported the nationalist cause. And what good Hungarian wouldn't want to, she thought, as the red, white and green flags fluttered in the breeze. There were families holding hands and groups of young people laughing and drinking. It was a scene that resonated with pride, and Morgan certainly understood the attraction of nationalism. After all, who didn't want to be proud of their own country?

She looked around for Berényi but the crowd was thick, moving through the park slowly, and there was no sign of him. Around the edges, Morgan could see groups of men with hard faces and fists that clenched plastic tumblers of beer. They wore the uniform of the civilian militia, officially dissolved by the Hungarian courts, but tolerated, and even encouraged, by many who supported their cause. The black uniform and caps evoked pictures that Morgan had seen in Yad Vashem, the Holocaust Museum, in Jerusalem. She knew that psychological research had shown that a uniform cloaked the individual in collective responsibility, and it was the best way to get people to obey authority figures and overcome their natural reticence to hurt others. She had read reports of the militia's torch-lit marches around Roma communities, creating terror in the persecuted group and even causing some to be evacuated for fear of explosive violence. It wouldn't take much to encourage this lot to attack the synagogue in revenge for the outrage of the Holy Right.

Morgan entered the gates and moved with the crowd into the park. It was a strange throwback to the Communist era, with huge statues of famous figures like Lenin, Marx and Engels as well as the boots of Stalin, all that remained of the dictator's statue, torn down in the 1956 revolution. Nearby, the Liberation Army Soldier stood six meters tall, striding with fists raised towards the enemy, shouting for revolution. The park was meant to be a reminder of the fall of Communism, but Morgan felt it somehow glorified those dark days, its propaganda now serving a modern purpose.

The open plan park was designed in six circles surrounding a central seventh, with the Communist star in the very middle. A dais had been set up there, but the focus of the crowd was on a large stage near the back of the park where a band was playing folk rock. As Morgan slid through the throng, she could see that some of those massed in front of the band had their right arms raised in a Fascist salute. No one seemed to care, and again, Morgan felt that she was witnessing a flashback, or an alternate universe where the last seventy years had been but a dream.

Behind the band, large screens projected visions of Hungary's greatness, images of propaganda that the Communist regime would have been proud to call their own. The handsome face of László Vay smiled while he greeted housewives and kissed babies, as strong men shook his hand and pledged allegiance. The video switched to footage of the militia marching underneath the banner of the Turul, the mythical bird, representing power, strength and nobility. Morgan noticed that many in the crowd watched the images even if they ignored the music, and the press were gathered around the edges, interviewing people. She had to get the footage of the labyrinth up onto that screen.

Weaving through the crowd, Morgan smiled up at the leering men so they would let her pass. Women eyed her suspiciously and Morgan suspected that any violence here would be equal opportunity. The smell of sweat and beer intensified as she made it to the front of the crowd, who were now swaying and singing along to what must be a popular song.

Peering into the shadows at the side of the stage, Morgan tried to see where the video was controlled. There was a guy hunched over a several laptops and a mixing desk, earphones on his head. Next to the technician, she spotted Hollo Berényi, compulsively looking at his watch, clearly expecting László to arrive for his big speech any moment. He pulled out his smartphone and dialed, appearing to be swearing silently as it failed to be answered. He must assume that László was still underground, but he would be more concerned soon enough.

Morgan noticed the lead singer glance to the side of the stage and Berényi made a gesture to carry on, keep playing. So László was already late, and that meant she didn't have much time. If Berényi couldn't fire up this crowd, he might take his militia and attack the synagogue anyway. Morgan thought of little Ilona, and of the old woman, screaming as she relived past horrors.

Her phone buzzed in her pocket.

"We're out of the labyrinth," Georg's voice was halting as he tried to catch his breath. "We've dealt with the … package … and I've got Zoltan out and we're at a local doctor's. Where are you?"

"On location," Morgan said briefly. "I should have something for you in the next ten minutes. Will you be able to monitor when the feed goes active even if I can't call you?"

"Yes, if you can plug the USB in, I'll get a ping on my

phone and I can send the video. I'll be waiting."

Morgan considered her options. Berényi had seen her briefly on the boat but would he place her face on this day of chaos? She made her decision and ducked back out through the crowd towards the busy bar. She adjusted her clothes, pulling down her T-shirt to reveal a little more cleavage. Grabbing two beers, she headed back to the screen control desk, evading the attentions of several inebriated men along the way.

When she returned, Berényi had his back to her and was talking to three other men, their bulk barely covered by the tight-fitting black uniforms. A couple of them glanced at her as she approached and she raised the beers in fake inebriation, giving a cheeky smile before she bent to the man at the desk. After a second, they carried on their conversation, clearly thinking she was a groupie for the band, but Morgan knew that Berényi's eyes could fall on her any minute. She hoped that Georg was ready to initiate whatever he needed to do if she managed to get the USB key into the computer, because she was on the edge of potential trouble here.

The technician turned at her approach and said something in Hungarian. His tone indicated that she shouldn't be there, that he was busy, but Morgan saw his eyes take in her curves with barely concealed interest. He was fat and his skin was pockmarked, clearly not the most attractive member of the band's team. Perhaps he would take any chance of attention. She stepped in close and gave him the beer, smiling and turning with her back to Berényi, shielding the view of the mixing desk and hiding her face.

"I love the music," she said, mouthing the words, as the band segued into something more thrash metal than folk. "You must be so clever to work with the band."

"Oh, English," the man said, smiling in a way that made Morgan suspect that he had enjoyed the attentions of British groupies before. He patted his lap, pulling out the chair to make room for her. She swallowed her disgust and sat on his knee, using the chance to get a look at his setup. She felt a hot hand on her thigh as he indicated the computer system with pride.

"This ... most important for band," he said. She smiled and nodded, seemingly enthusiastic as he explained the setup in Hungarian, pleased to have someone share his passion. Morgan noticed a USB port on the side farthest from her, but she would need to stretch across him to plug it in. She felt his hand move up from her thigh, towards her breast, his breath hot on her neck.

Morgan fought the desire to get up and run, instead pressing forward into his hand. As he took the chance to feel her soft curves, she retrieved the USB key from her pocket. Palming it, she turned towards him, trying to glaze her eyes in a parody of drunken lust. She could hear the band winding up their song, the chorus on its third repetition. She bent her head, her lips meeting his and as he closed his eyes, she felt behind her for the USB port.

The man's thick tongue plundered Morgan's mouth, all sense of his job forgotten as he groped her breast with one hand and with the other pulled her firmly onto his stiffening crotch. Just one more second, Morgan thought, her body desperate to pull away as she tried to dock the USB key. She felt the click and she leaned away from the man, smiling coquettishly. He said something in Hungarian, no doubt some version of "let's go somewhere more private later," his hand never leaving her breast. Everything in Morgan screamed at her to use her Krav Maga close combat skills and get out of there, but she had to stay and make sure that the video was delivered.

She smiled again, nodding as if in agreement, glancing over his shoulder at the screen. Nothing had changed and the band played on, with the video of militant propaganda still playing in the background. Had something gone wrong?

"What are you doing here?" The voice was rough and heavily accented. Morgan felt a hand on her arm pull her away from the technician's lap. She found herself staring into the dark eyes of Hollo Berényi, his black hair shining, like an oil slick hiding the lifeless depths beneath.

CHAPTER 14

"I'M ON HOLIDAY," MORGAN said. "And I wanted to meet the band." She smiled at Berényi, forcing flirtation into her gaze, fully aware of what this man was capable of. "Are you part of the band?"

Morgan's senses were in overdrive. As Berényi's eyes assessed her, she could feel his men drawing in closer behind, their interest sparked by her lewd behavior with the technician. She needed to get out of there, but so far, there was no change on the screen. Had the USB stick not been pushed in far enough?

"I've seen you before," Berényi said, suspicion growing in his eyes and an edge of menace creeping into his voice. "What are you really doing here?"

The crowd started chanting as the band led them in another popular song, the chorus some kind of repetitive rant. But then the sound faltered, tailing off into silence as the giant screens flickered from the nationalist symbols to the view of a cavern lit by candlelight.

Berényi noticed the change of mood and turned from Morgan towards the screen, his eyes widening as he saw the táltos cutting a piece of the Holy Right, and the face of László Vay rapt with wonder as he knelt to receive the dark Mass.

Morgan took her chance to slip towards the barrier, but

as she moved away, Berényi spun and caught her arm.

"You," he hissed. "Jew bitch."

He barked something in Hungarian and two of his men rushed forward to hold her as Morgan struggled to escape. She slipped from one grip, defending herself, but the other man caught her from behind. One meaty hand covered her mouth to quiet her, and her heart raced as she knew it was only a matter of time until Berényi would deal with her himself. She was pulled tight against the hard body of one of the guards, waiting for the order. She gathered her strength, focusing on the weak points of the man behind, her mind recalling her training in the Israeli Defense Force.

The technician was frantically tapping at the computer, clearly unable to gain control of the screens again. He spotted the USB stick and pulled it from the side but the video kept on playing, a loop clearly focused on the Holy Right and Vay drinking the tainted wine. From her pinioned position, Morgan could see disgust dawning on the face of the crowd as Hungary's golden boy showed his true colors. The press were filming and Morgan had no doubt that this was going out on national television, that the radio waves would be alive with gossip, and social media would be spreading the word. Some in the crowd held up their phones, recording the images and in this age of connectivity, there would be nowhere to hide from this scandal. Vay's disappearance would be taken as a response to public shame, and he would be forgotten.

Berényi spun from the technician's desk, and Morgan could see indecision in his eyes. Should he go on stage now and take control for his party? Or should he disappear before he was tainted with the same disgrace? He walked toward her, and she could see in his eyes that he would make her pay for this outrage. He nodded at the men and they started pulling her backwards towards the curtained area behind the stage. It had to be now.

Morgan bit the man's hand, tearing at his flesh as she bent forward hard, shifting her centre of gravity so that the man was pulled over her. At the same time, she stomped back with her boot, raking the side of his calf. That opened up enough space for her arm to swing back and hit him once, twice, in the groin, all in a matter of a second. He grunted and let her go, clearly not expecting such resistance. Morgan spun away, arms raised in the open palm Krav Maga stance. She saw the other men pull batons from their waist pouches, flicking them to full length. Morgan knew that she couldn't hold off this many, but she was determined not to go easily.

The men advanced and then, suddenly, Berényi barked an order and they stopped. Morgan looked around to see two news crews filming them from the crowd, now focused on the drama unfolding around her. It was as if the real world had suddenly flooded into Hollo Berényi's consciousness. He knew that there were too many witnesses to what he wanted to do and he wasn't going down like his boss.

The reporters called out to him, wanting a statement, but he spun away, walking quickly behind the stage followed by his men. The technician ran out after them, followed by the tenacious media, and soon Morgan was left alone at the side of the stage. The band members left sheepishly and the crowd began to disperse, the energy of the day sucked dry by the revelations of the video feed. There was an air of anti-climax, as the tension dissipated into gossip and the planned riot was forgotten. Morgan knew that the danger was over, at least for today.

CHAPTER 15

MORGAN SAT ON THE steps of the synagogue, watching as a team from the local community swept up the broken glass and picked up the piles of rubbish. The Eröszak party was in disarray and the relic returned to the Basilica, so a tentative calm had descended on the city. A woman sang softly as she worked, a melody that Morgan recognized as a tune her father used to hum. It was a song of hope and resurrection that Jews had sung as they recovered from disaster in their long history. There was great pride in the woman's cleaning, an attitude of prayer in her work, as if God saw her service.

Zoltan came out from the doors behind her, his body stiff and arm in a sling.

"Many Hungarian Jews have fled the country, but these people won't leave," he said. "This is their home and mine, despite its dangers. And I will stay to help them, because it's not over, Morgan. It will never be over while the mob is only one degree away from violence."

Morgan knew that his words were true, for she had seen it for herself in the eyes of the people at Memento Park as well as all over the world on her travels.

"You know where I stand, Zoltan," she said, reaching for his hand and squeezing it. "Your people are my people and that is my truth, regardless of what others might say. I wasn't born Jewish, but a part of my heart lies in Jerusalem, and now a part lies here."

Zoltan looked at her, and she saw past the scars to the man within. One day he would die in defense of justice. She knew that, and he probably did too, but his loyalty was to the downtrodden, to those who could not defend themselves. Morgan felt a spark of recognition, as she knew that there was a part of her that felt the same, but the ARKANE team was fast becoming her family, and she needed to get back to join them.

She stood up, brushing the dust from her jeans. Zoltan held out his hand to shake hers.

"You always have a place here, Morgan. And if you ever need me, I'll come."

She ignored his hand, leaning forward to kiss his scarred cheek. His fingertips briefly touched her back, and as she hugged him, she felt his stiffness relent and he embraced her in return. At last, she pulled away, smiling.

"I'll see you again, Zoltan. I'm sure of it."

Morgan walked out of the Dohany Street synagogue and into the waiting taxi, heading back to the airport and ARKANE.

***

As the car sped along, Morgan sat quietly for a moment, staring out at the same streets that she had passed so early this morning. Could it really have only been one day? It seemed that so much had happened.

She sighed, finally turning her ARKANE cellphone back on, ready to return to her real world. There were several text messages from Martin Klein, the genius head archivist. The first text contained her updated flight information, but the second made her heart race. *There's a strange package waiting for you. The writing is faded and the sender is noted as Leon Sierra.* But how could that be, she wondered. It was her father's name and he had died several years ago, blown apart by a suicide bomber in Beersheba. Morgan was suddenly keen to get back and find out what was in the impossible package.

Thanks for joining Morgan and the ARKANE team!

If you loved the book and have a moment to spare,
I would really appreciate a short review where you
bought the book. Your help in spreading the word is
gratefully appreciated.

You can also get a free copy of the bestselling ARKANE
thriller, *Day of the Vikings*, when you sign up to join my
Reader's Group at:

WWW.JFPENN.COM/FREEBOOK

**More books in the international bestselling
ARKANE thriller series. Described by readers as
'Dan Brown meets Lara Croft.'**
Available in print, ebook and audio formats
at all online stores.

Stone of Fire #1
Crypt of Bone #2
Ark of Blood #3
One Day in Budapest #4
Day of the Vikings #5
Gates of Hell #6
One Day in New York #7
Destroyer of Worlds #8
End of Days #9

The London Psychic Series. Described by readers as 'the love child of Stephen King and PD James.'
Available in ebook, print and audio formats.

Desecration
Delirium
Deviance

A Thousand Fiendish Angels, short stories inspired by Dante's Inferno, on the edge of thriller and the occult.

Risen Gods

WWW.JFPENN.COM

AUTHOR'S NOTE

This novella is a work of fiction, but the inspiration for it comes from actual events and real places.

I visited Budapest in November 2012 and was deeply affected by the horrific layers of history that the city has endured. The Dohany Street Synagogue and the House of Terror were devastating, and once I saw the Holy Hand of St Istvan in the Basilica, I knew what the crux of my story would be. I wanted to give a taste of the grand city in the book but also evoke visions of a day that seemed all too possible given the political situation. Here are some of my sources if you want to investigate further.

Rise of right-wing nationalism in Hungary

We like to think that the horrors of World War II couldn't happen again, that we are too educated to succumb to ultra-nationalism or the persecution of minorities, that those things happen in other countries, to other people. But that belief is fiction.

In December 2012, Hungary's far-right Jobbik party called for lists of prominent Jews to be drawn up to "protect national security" bit.ly/14zRbCL . Anti-Semitic violence is growing in Eastern Europe reut.rs/SARA1x and in the wake of the European financial crisis and austerity measures, far right-wing parties are gaining popularity. European genocide happened as recently as the Bosnian War in the 1990s, so we can't believe that such violence remains in the past or just in 'other' areas of the world. With this novella, I wanted to highlight the disturbing political situation, as well as the dark history of Budapest, whose people who have suffered so much.

For more, see the following resources:

'My week with Hungary's Far Right' by Brian Whelan: bit.ly/12TivWS

You can watch part of the video documentary here: bit.ly/13PmB1u

Official terror for Hungary's Roma: bit.ly/AAHJLT

Jewish community in Budapest

The Gold Train and settlement are true bit.ly/177Shl8 but of course the involvement of ARKANE and the return of the painting is fictional.

You can read more about the Dohany Street Synagogue, the mass grave and the ghetto here: www.greatsynagogue.hu

The Shoes of the Danube memorial: bit.ly/8hTopj

Other Budapest City Landmarks

All of the landmarks described in the city of Budapest do exist, although the events described in the book are of course fiction.

You can see some of my photos and other pictures here: www.pinterest.com/jfpenn/budapest/

The House of Terror is an incredible museum now, with the cells as described and rooms full of secret police memorabilia, as well as stories of those lost. www.terrorhaza.hu

There really is a labyrinth under Castle Hill that was closed to the public in 2011 under strange circumstances. I have taken liberties with the internal geography, as I couldn't visit, but you can watch a video on their website that gives you a sense of the place: www.labirintus.com/en/1003/gallery

The Memento Park is full of large statues, a memorial to Communism www.mementopark.hu

ABOUT J.F. PENN

JOANNA PENN IS THE New York Times and USA Today bestselling author of thrillers on the edge. Joanna has a Master's degree in Theology from the University of Oxford, Mansfield College and a Graduate Diploma in Psychology from the University of Auckland, New Zealand.

She lives in London, England but spent eleven years in Australia and New Zealand. Joanna worked for thirteen years as an international business consultant within the IT industry, but is now a full-time author-entrepreneur. She is the author of the ARKANE series, the London Psychic series and other books in the action-adventure and thriller genre.

Joanna is a PADI Divemaster and enjoys traveling as often as possible. She loves to read, drink Pinot Noir and soak up European culture through art, architecture and food.

You can get a free book as well as notification of new books and giveaways at:
www.JFPenn.com/freebook

Connect with Joanna online:

(e) joanna@JFPenn.com
(w) www.JFPenn.com
(t) @thecreativepenn
(f) www.facebook.com/JFPennAuthor
www.pinterest.com/jfpenn/

Joanna Penn also writes non-fiction. Available in print, ebook and audiobook formats.

Career Change: Stop hating your job, discover what you really want to do, and start doing it!

How To Market A Book

Public Speaking For Authors, Creatives and Other Introverts

Business for Authors: How to be an Author Entrepreneur

For writers:

Joanna's site www.TheCreativePenn.com helps people write, publish and market their books through articles, audio, video and online products as well as live workshops. Joanna is available internationally for speaking events aimed at writers, authors and entrepreneurs. Joanna also has a popular podcast for writers on iTunes, The Creative Penn.

ACKNOWLEDGEMENTS

As always, my love and thanks to Jonathan, my first reader and wonderful husband. And a huge thank you to my readers, I hope that this book has both entertained you and made you think.

Thanks to my line editor, Jacqueline Penn, who keeps me on my toes with her insightful challenges. Thanks to author TJ Cooke, www.TJCooke.com for his suggestion of the Memorial Park, which turned out to be a great setting for the final scene. Thanks to Meg Tufano for her fantastically detailed beta-reading.

Thanks as ever to my cover designer, Derek Murphy from bookcovers.creativindie.com who did another fantastic job and to Liz Broomfield from Libroediting.com for proof-reading the final draft. Thanks to Jane Dixon Smith www.jdsmith-design.com for the interior formatting.

CPSIA information can be obtained
at www.ICGtesting.com
Printed in the USA
LVOW11s0633030517
532940LV00003B/607/P